INTENTIONS

For Sarah—
Here's to living with intention!

DEBORAH HEILIGMAN

Deborah Heiligman

INTENTIONS

October 29, 2013

EMBER

This is a work of fiction. Names, characters, places, and incidents either are the product of the author's imagination or are used fictitiously. Any resemblance to actual persons, living or dead, events, or locales is entirely coincidental.

Text copyright © 2012 by Deborah Heiligman
Cover art copyright © 2012 by iStockphoto.com/JJRD

All rights reserved. Published in the United States by Ember, an imprint of Random House Children's Books, a division of Random House, Inc., New York. Originally published in hardcover in the United States by Alfred A. Knopf, an imprint of Random House Children's Books, New York, in 2012.

Ember and the E colophon are registered trademarks of Random House, Inc.

Visit us on the Web! randomhouse.com/teens

Educators and librarians, for a variety of teaching tools, visit us at RHTeachersLibrarians.com

The Library of Congress has cataloged the hardcover edition of this work as follows:
Heiligman, Deborah.
Intentions / Deborah Heiligman. — 1st ed.
p. cm.
Summary: After fifteen-year-old Rachel overhears her rabbi committing infidelity, she must come to terms with the fact that adults make mistakes, too—and that she is old enough to be held responsible for her own mistakes.
ISBN 978-0-375-86861-0 (trade) — ISBN 978-0-375-96861-7 (lib. bdg.) — ISBN 978-0-375-89933-1 (ebook)
[1. Coming of age—Fiction. 2. Responsibility—Fiction. 3. Jews—United States—Fiction.]
I. Title.
PZ7.H3673In 2012 [E]—dc23 2011026667

ISBN 978-0-375-87242-6 (tr. pbk.)

Printed in the United States of America

10 9 8 7 6 5 4 3 2 1

First Ember Edition 2013

Random House Children's Books supports the First Amendment and celebrates the right to read.

For the kids in the photo on the wall

CONTENTS

The Sanctuary, Now 1
1. The Sanctuary 3
2. Refuge 7
3. Intention 10
4. Hell 19
5. Don't Let the Goddamn Sun Shine 23
6. Not Like a Virgin 31
6a. Not a Virgin 38
7. Devil's Food Cake 'n' Coffee Man, Man 40
8. The Morning After 48
9. Kissing Elephants 55
10. Sloppy 61
11. Streamers 70
12. Union 78
13. Barefoot and in the Kitchen 86
14. Trumped 92
15. Action, Action, We Want Action! 102
16. To Have and Have Not 111
17. Blah, Blah, Blah 123
18. Kissing Elephants II 129
19. The Punch Line 134
20. Party Animal 140

21. A Little Bomb 155
22. Table for One 162
23. Locked Out 167
24. Almost Amish 172
25. *Tikkun Olam* 177
26. Flooding 185
27. Going Backward 198
28. Going Backward II 204
28a. Going Backward III 206
29. Lightning 210
29a. Lightning II 213
30. Flying Solo 215
31. Everything I Need to Know I Learned In . . . 220
32. Going Down(town) 228
33. Bursting 234
34. Out of Breath 240
35. New Leaf 249
36. The Sanctuary 256
The Sanctuary, Now 259

The Sanctuary, Now

I get out of the car and look at the building.

It's been more than a decade since I set foot in there—since I was sixteen and left this town.

I'm scared to go in. But here I am, and here I go.

These steps used to seem so steep, but in no time I am at the front of my old temple. The door is as heavy as I remembered. A lion carved in the wood seems to roar at me as I struggle with the weight.

Inside I head straight for the sanctuary, my footsteps echoing.

Just as it was back then, that evening before confirmation class, the sanctuary is dark.

I stand in the shadows for a minute, and then I flick on the lights. This time I want to see it all.

CHAPTER 1

THE SANCTUARY

"I am so out of here!" I yell, letting the door slam behind me. They're too busy fighting to notice I'm gone, I'm sure. In an hour, when it's time to drive me to temple, they'll be looking for me—"Rachel? Rachel?" Yeah, guys, remember me?

God. Could they have been any more awful to each other at dinner? I inhaled my food so fast I didn't taste a bite. A pasta and peas vacuum cleaner.

I run and run until I pretty much can't breathe. I'm sure I'm going to puke. What is the opposite of a vacuum cleaner? I slow way down so I don't become whatever that is. Catch my breath. Yeah, walking might be a better idea.

I am so sick of their stupid fights, I don't know what to do. Maybe I'll talk to the rabbi about my parents.

Middle-aged, nerdy, bushy-bearded, potbellied, Jewish Santa Claus–looking Rabbi Cohn. Yup. He's just that wise, kind, brilliant. If anyone can make me feel better, it's him. He might be the most perfect human being on the planet.

I walk through the parking lot to the back door, but it's still locked. It is early—forty-five minutes before class is supposed to start. So I go around to the front, pull open the heavy wooden door. The lobby is empty, but the lights are on. I hope he's here early tonight, in the sanctuary like he sometimes is before class, getting the Torah ready for the Saturday service.

But the sanctuary is dark, quiet, empty.

Oh well. It'll be good to have time to myself. I don't turn on the light; I want the dark. I run my hand along the top of the back row. The feel of the smooth, polished wood is soothing. I sit down a few seats in from the door and just breathe.

What would it be like if they got divorced? They never used to fight. Alexis always said my parents were the happiest couple in the world. Now they seem absolutely miserable. With no brothers or sisters to stick with me, I can see myself as a little Rachel ball being ping-ponged back and forth between them. Or, worse, maybe, left with just one of them, like Alexis.

Alexis. God. Ever since she came back from her dad's, a diamond stud in her nose, her black curls that used to be just like mine turned into bleached-blond spikes, smoking cigarettes and weed, bragging about having sex with her twenty-year-old boyfriend, I've felt . . . abandoned. Sometimes she is the same smart, funny, loving-me-better-than-anyone best friend, but then without any warning she'll get distant and cool. She is definitely in charge of our relationship now. I have no idea what I can talk to her about and what I can't.

Every time I try to talk to her about my parents, she puts that wall up. I haven't even tried to ask her about Jake. She'd just make a crack about my being *young*.

Oh God. I need to stop thinking. I need just to BE. In my

peaceful sanctuary. I have so many good memories of this place—and one sad one.

Grandpa's coffin right in front of the *bima*. I can still see it, in my mind's eye, though I try not to. God it was an awful day. But the rabbi was perfect. Right before the funeral service, the family met in his office. He pinned ripped black ribbons onto our clothes—the sign that we were in mourning. Spoke about what a great man my grandpa was, how he had lived a happy life with Grandma. And then, as we were walking out of his office, the rabbi said, quietly, just to me, "He was so proud of you, Rachel," and I burst into tears. It was exactly what I needed to hear.

As I sit here with my head back, staring at the ceiling—or what I can see of it with the lights off—I try to think what the rabbi would say about my parents. I try to channel his wisdom, but instead of channeling anything, I fall asleep.

I wake up because I hear noises. I am not alone.

What am I hearing? Small, soft sounds. Whispers. I slowly open my eyes, wait for them to adjust to the darkness. I sit up and look around. But I don't see anyone. For some reason I know not to stand up, cough, make myself known.

Then the sounds start getting louder. I can't quite tell what they are—or I am not ready to admit it. It isn't exactly people talking, but I can tell there are two people. A low voice, and a higher voice. Groans. Sighs. Moans.

Holy crap. Who is it? Who could it be? Having *sex* in the sanctuary! For God's sake! It seems like the sounds are coming from the *bima*—the rabbi's *bima*—where he leads services; where the birthday kids go up for their blessing every month, the rabbi holding his hands above them, fingers spread to let in God; where I stood in front of the congregation almost three years ago, when I was thirteen, with my mother and grandmother as we passed the Torah from generation to generation.

It is so tacky, so sacrilegious.

I am dying to know who it is.

And then I hear them. Two words. Just two words. And the instant I hear them, those two words change everything I know to be true. Those two words become my personal torture, the hot secret I will carry with me like the burning coal that singed the tongue of toddler Moses.

And then she says them again:

"OH, RABBI."

CHAPTER 2

REFUGE

Before those two words, I thought that most people were basically good, and I was sure that holy people were, well, holy.

I just had the crap beat out of that stupid idea.

"Oh God," the woman cries. "Oh, Rabbi."

I am going to puke.

"Oh God," he says. "Oh yes."

Oh God. I really *am* going to puke. I have to get out of here. Without them—who is she?—without them seeing me. Maybe it's the rabbi's wife. That's not so bad, right? It's disgusting, but also kind of romantic. Making love in the synagogue, it could be a spiritual experience. But then I realize—duh!—Mrs. Cohn definitely would not say "Oh, Rabbi" in the throes of passion.

I don't know a lot, but I know that.

I slide down farther in my seat and onto the floor. I get on all fours and start to crawl. I am a pacifist and I hate war movies, but all I can think about is those scenes when soldiers crawl on the ground, their faces covered in mud so they can't be seen. I can't be seen. How will I get up and open the door?

But then I realize that this is not a problem. They are so busy, so very, VERY busy, doing what they're doing, they probably wouldn't hear a nuclear bomb go off. Do nuclear bombs even make noise?

Rachel, get yourself out of here.

I stand up, open the door a crack so I can slip out, then close it slowly and quietly, just in case. I make a mad dash down the hallway, into the bathroom, plop down on the couch in the sitting area for one second, and then race into a stall and heave. I want to stop myself, but I can't.

I am sweating and shaking.

I almost cry, but if I start, I won't ever stop. I'll wash my face. I'll rinse out my mouth. I'm about to leave the stall when I hear the outer bathroom door open.

I back up and quietly close the stall door. It's *her*. I know it.

And then it's impossible not to know it's *her*, because she's crying and saying over and over again, "What have I done? What have I done?" I make sure the stall door is locked and climb onto the toilet seat so she won't see my feet. I surprise myself at my quick thinking. I used to wonder how I'd act in a crisis and now I know: first I throw up, then I climb onto a toilet seat.

I wonder how long I'm going to have to stay here like this when my phone starts to vibrate in my pocket. Shit! Probably my parents: WHERE ARE YOU?

I grab on to the wall to steady myself. I try to hold my breath.

Then I think, wait a minute, why is she crying? I've been assuming that she seduced him, that she's an evil woman who besmirched my darling hero of a rabbi. But if that is so, why is she sobbing, "How can I get married now? How can I get married *here* now? Oh my God! What have I done?"

She has a strong Southern accent, completely out of place here in Pennsylvania. And then I get it: she is marrying someone who grew up here. They're getting married at the temple. And she came to meet the rabbi, to get to know him. Boy, did she.

And so did I.

CHAPTER 3

INTENTION

"*Shalom*, everyone," the rabbi says. He beams at us with those sparkling dark eyes of his, and holds up his hands, palms down, as if to bless us.

I want to hurl things at him—words, shoes, vomit.

But everyone else is answering him back, "*Shalom*, Rabbi." I turn around. They're all gazing at him the same way: with respect, adoration, and love—mixed with a little embarrassment, though, because kids our age aren't supposed to feel this way about adults. The only ones who aren't looking at him with adoration are Alexis, who seems to be sleeping, and Adam, the rabbi's son. He's glaring.

And so am I. Rachel Greenberg, the former rabbi-adorer, is now
sick to her stomach with rage
and disgust.

And stuck in the front row because I got to class late, having stayed hidden in the stall until Crying Bride left. Then I cleaned myself up, reassured my parents that I was alive and well (my first lie), and snuck into class right before the rabbi. Of course he was late. He probably had to, I don't know, go to rabbi confession or something. Nah, he probably just took a shower.

I wonder what *she* did when she got back to wherever she was going. She probably threw herself into a scalding tub. No, into a *mikvah*! For purity. Ha. I must have laughed out loud, because the rabbi clears his throat and looks right at me.

Why did I come to class? What was I thinking?

"Tonight we're going to talk about prayer, about how to pray. And then, after the break, we'll go into the sanctuary—"

Are you kidding me, you creep? Return to the scene of the crime?

"—and pray, with *kavanah*, with intention." He pauses and looks out at all of us, one at a time, catching each of our eyes. I try to avoid meeting his but I can't, and as I look into his eyes, I doubt myself. Doubt what I heard. Doubt what I think he did. But then my stomach roils, as if my stomach brain—we have a kind of brain in our stomachs! I learned this in science class!—knows better than my other brain.

I look down at the floor, nauseated. The tiles are black and white, but they seem gray.

Gray. Not black and white.

Maybe it *wasn't* what it seemed.

"Rachel, Rachel, are you there?"

What?

"Did you hear what I asked you?" the rabbi says.

I shake my head, not trusting my voice.

"I asked what you think about when you pray."

I shrug my shoulders, stare at the blackboard behind him.

He sighs, loudly, and continues. "Class. You think you already know how to pray, and in one sense you do. When we pray, first we have to learn how to do it—the words of the prayers, what they mean, in what order to say each line, and in which order to say the prayers. You already know all of that. That's called *keva*."

I look up because in spite of it all I'm interested.

He pauses, looks at us. We know the drill. Everyone says "*keva*." Even me.

Shit, I can't believe he got me back on his side.

How can I sit here and listen to him? Pretend nothing happened? Because I know something did.

"It is important to pray with *keva*," he says. "But to really reach God we need to pray with *kavanah*, with intention. What do you think I mean by that?"

He looks at me. Of course me. This is exactly the kind of thing I love to talk about. Not anymore. Tonight I want to spear him in the heart with a hot poker. Oh wait, *he* is the hot poker. I crack myself up. I am so funny I should take it onstage.

"Rachel, is this funny to you?"

Might as well go with it. "A little funny, yeah," I say.

There are sounds of approval in back of me. "Dude!" someone says.

I turn around. Adam. He's smiling at me, not his usual half smile, but a big full-on grin. And he's wiggling his eyebrows. Next to him in the back row, Alexis has a look of—can it be?—admiration.

But when I turn back, Jacob Schmidt, Jake, my almost boyfriend, sitting a couple of chairs away from me, is frowning. He raises *his* eyebrows in a question. We were friends when we were little, and ever since he moved back to town a year ago I've wondered if we could be more. Lately, we've been flirting like mad. But it's getting kind of intense, and I'm not sure I'm ready.

I turn back to the rabbi and give him a dirty look only he can see. He looks at me, confused. And then I give it to him.

"Oh, Rabbi," I say. "Did I offend you? It was not my *intention*."

He winces.

Before the rabbi can say anything, Jake speaks—I'm sure to save me. "Do you mean by 'intention' that we have to give the prayers our full attention?" He emphasizes the *a* in *attention*: UHtention. He looks at me. I give him a smile. I'm dying inside because of the stupid rabbi, but Jake just makes me smile. He's so smart. He's handsome. He's intense. I love that intensity of his. But maybe he's too Good. Maybe he's a nerd. That did sound a little nerdy. UHtention.

I groan. Aloud.

"Rachel, why don't you go out into the hall until you can pull yourself together?" the rabbi says, and now—I can't help it—I feel like crap.

"Sorry," I say. "Bad day. I'll calm down." I give a little smile to him, and to Jake—they are both looking at me with the same exact expression, I swear: disappointment, relief, and hope.

The rabbi says softly, "Thank you," and smiles, and I want to die. I should want to kill him. I *should* want to tell everyone what he did so he will be known for what he really is, so he will be humiliated, kicked out, drawn and quartered, tarred and feathered, hung by his— What *do* you do to a Bad Rabbi? But instead I look up and try to count the squares of tile on the ceiling. There are too many, and I lose count. But at least I make it through the first half of class without getting myself into more trouble.

During the fifteen-minute break, Jake and some of the other boys usually play basketball in the playground with the rabbi. I love to watch them, especially Jake. Because he's a swimmer, he's lean, and strong, and when he jumps up and gets that ball into the net, I want to know what his back feels like at that moment. I'm kind of hung up on his back. I wonder if that's weird.

But seeing the rabbi joke around with them tonight as if he hadn't just . . . I couldn't stand it.

I need to tell someone what I heard. If I could get Jake away from the basketball game, I would. But maybe he wouldn't believe me. Also, how awkward would that be? I'd have to talk about sex—yeah, no way.

I can't tell Adam, that's for sure. It's his father. I look at the other girls in the class. I've known most of them for years, but I'm not close to any of them. I come back to Alexis. She's my only option. I have to try.

"Nice sweater, Raebee," she says to me now. I forget what I'm wearing. Oh, that new sweater Mom got me.

"Thanks," I say.

"You always look so great in red." She smiles. It's a good Alexis moment!

"Thanks!" I say again, this time my eyes welling up for some reason, though honestly I'm not sure if she's being sincere or sarcastic.

"Come with us?" she says, and I quickly say, "OK!"

I glance back at Jake and then walk down the hill to the

Wawa with Alexis and Adam and some of the other kids. They go to get candy, get away. Maybe I should put something in my stomach, since I threw up my whole dinner. Pretzels.

I watch Alexis walking ahead of me. She doesn't notice I'm not next to her. Now that my parents are so not "the happiest couple in the world," I can imagine how depressing it's been for her. Her house used to be so full of life. She loved coming to mine because it was calm, but I loved going to her house because it wasn't. In my house the walls are beige. Dinner is always at six o'clock, and the food is *fine*. At her house there are bright colors everywhere, and back in the day, you never knew when there would be a real meal, but you could count on something exotic to try—popcorn made in truffle oil, anchovy paste on homemade crackers, dark chocolate sea-salt caramels dipped in peanut butter. Her brothers were loud and obnoxious and teased us mercilessly, but they also let us in on the secrets of the world, because they're so much older. Alexis's mom and dad, who insisted I call them Mark and Ginny, talked all the time about politics, books, relatives, neighbors. They argued, too, now that I think about it, but the fighting seemed like it was a natural part of the mix.

Alexis and I had sleepovers every weekend, and no matter which house we stayed at, we were happy.

Then, last year, we started spending most weekends at my house. I didn't know why, and when I asked her, she just shrugged. I still don't understand why she never told me that her parents were having trouble. I'm dying to talk to her about mine. The first I knew her folks had split up was when her dad moved into that crummy little apartment behind the Wegmans. We had one sleepover there, and it was so awkward and strange, with Alexis and me sharing a twin bed, head to toe, because her dad didn't have two spare beds. When he took us out for dinner at a Chinese restaurant, the three of us sat there with nothing to say. I thought her heart would break when he moved all the way to California suddenly last spring; her older brothers were already living there. Now she can see her dad only in the summer. Her mom got a puppy, but a dog can't fill up all those empty, silent rooms. I haven't slept there since, and Lex never wants to come over to my house anymore.

I look at her walking ahead of me now, and I know what she's been through, or close to it.

I walk faster to catch up.

"Hey, Alexis," I say. I bravely loop my arm through hers. Adam's on her other side.

"You really got to my dad tonight," he says with a smile. "Way to go."

"Yeah, you're usually such a suck-up," says Alexis, pulling away her arm. "I was shocked, shocked!" she laughs, putting her hand to her head in a dramatic gesture. She grabs Adam, and the two of them dash into the store ahead of me.

I feel sick. I just can't figure her out.

Does she like Adam? I doubt she's going to stay with the guy in California. And Adam *is* hot. OH, wait a minute. . . . It never made sense to me that Adam was the rabbi's son. Not until tonight. I always thought, how could such a good guy have a bad-boy son?

Adam's always been a rebel, especially in Sunday school. And since we got to high school, there have been all these rumors about him: that he deals pot, that he sleeps around with girls *and* boys, that he had an affair with a student teacher. I don't really believe all that stuff. But he *is* hot, and it's easy to see how he could get pretty much any girl or boy he wanted.

Like his dad? Oh God. (Oh, Rabbi!)

The weird thing is, Adam looks like his father. He lifts weights and wrestles, so he's buff, not chubby, but they do look alike. God, poor Mrs. Cohn. She's the straightest, sweetest, most innocent lady I know. I think. What do I know?

I need to make sense of this. I need food.

I walk in and head straight for the pretzels. While I'm at it, I grab some Twizzlers and a Snickers, too. I'm walking over to the sodas to get not a ginger ale but a Diet (oh, the irony) Coke when I see Alexis and Adam stuffing Peanut Butter Kandy Kakes, my favorite, under their jackets. I get a sinking feeling in the pit of my stomach and quickly walk away. Other kids are in line; I go stand behind Marissa.

"Hi," I say to her.

"Hey," she says to me. "What's up?"

Then Adam comes over to me, leans close, and says, "Hey, Ronderful Rachel." Then he whispers right into my ear, giving me chills. "Why are you *paying* for that stuff, honey?"

Alexis comes over to my other side, starts playing with my hair. I sigh. Why does it feel so good to have someone play with your hair?

"Sometimes I miss mine," she says.

"Grow it again!"

"Nah," she says, grabbing my arm and yanking me out of line. "Stuff it under your shirt. Don't pay, Raebee."

Why has she started using my nickname again all of a sudden? Until tonight, she hadn't used it since—since forever. But there is no way I'm going to shoplift junk food. My world may not be golden anymore, but I'm not going to turn it into shit. Or some such metaphor.

Just then the door opens and a really cute guy walks in, probably from the college. He's not at all my type—or what I thought was my type—he's tall, blond, Nordic-looking. Definitely not Jewish. His ancestors probably murdered my ancestors. I must be staring right at him, because he stares right at me. I feel bold, crazy.

"How you doing?" he says.

And as if I'm in a movie, I say, "I'd be doing better if you'd come closer."

He laughs and leans in toward me, and I reach up and kiss him on the lips. He grabs me and gives me the longest and most delicious kiss in the world. Then he has his hands up my shirt and I have mine down his pants and—

OK, none of that really happens except in my weird little mind.

What really happens is he says, "How you doing?" and I say, "Fine," and then I back away from him, smack into the rack holding chips and pretzels. It comes tumbling down with a clatter and a crash.

I run out of the Wawa (without paying for my stuff—only I won't realize that until much later) and back to the temple. I head right to "my" bathroom and decide to hide in there until class is over. There is no way I am going into that sanctuary again tonight.

CHAPTER 4

HELL

I'm sure from the outside it looks like I'm just a normal teenage girl sitting on the temple steps waiting for her mother to pick her up. From the inside it feels like I am a teenager in hell.

My own personal, personally designed hell.

According to His Holiness, Jews don't believe in the kind of hell Christians believe in.

Back when we were sitting *shivah* at Grandma's, I asked him about it. For seven days after the funeral, we stayed at Grandma and Grandpa's house, her real house, not the complex where she lives now so she can be on one floor and surrounded by neighbors. Mom, Dad, Mom's brother, Uncle Joe, and his wife, Aunt Paula, and my cousins and I hung out all day.

Every evening, people came to visit (bringing food, so much food!), and the rabbi led a short service. It was pretty nice, spending that much time with my family, but I was really sad about losing Grandpa. He was my, I don't know, my anchor—I always felt so loved and *seen* by him.

I clung to the hope that I would see him again one day in heaven, even though I was pretty sure that was a Christian thing, not a Jewish thing. But I desperately wanted to believe it, so one night I asked the rabbi if Jews believe in heaven.

We were sitting on Grandma's window seat, watching people get into their cars. The rabbi smiled sadly and said most Jews don't believe in a heaven where you can see people again. He said that Grandpa would live on in my memories. It wasn't at all what I wanted to hear, and I started to cry. He said, "It is up to you to keep his memory alive, Rachel. Talk about him with your family, tell stories about him, even write about him." That didn't make me feel as good as if he had said, "Sure, you'll see him again!" But it was something.

Then he said, "This will be a hard time for you. But you will be OK, Rachel. You will." And I cried again, not because I was *more* upset, but because he understood.

"What about hell?" I'd blurted out.

He said there were different ideas about hell. He told me his two favorites. One is that the afterlife is a place where you listen to Torah all day, and if you are in heaven you love that, and if you are in hell, you hate it. The other is that the afterlife is a huge and delicious meal but people can't bend their elbows to feed themselves. In heaven they feed each other. In hell everyone stares at the food, starving and salivating.

As I wait for my mother to pick me up now, I know I'm in hell. I can't hold this secret inside any longer. Two hours and it's killing me. And probably I am *supposed* to tell someone. Aren't I? Mom will know what to do. She's a social worker.

Why is she taking so long to get here? I am mad at her for taking so long. No. I'm mad at her for fighting with my dad so much lately. Really mad.

But in spite of my anger, when I see Mom pull up in the Prius, her brand-new, treasured car, I smile. She worked hard to get that car, saving up her own money so it would be hers, all hers. And she keeps it cleaner than anything else in her life. We're both slobs.

It hits me smack in my heart: I love my mom. As much as this surprises me, it is exactly what I'm feeling. *I love my mom*.

I sprint to the car, like I'm sure the foster kids do when she goes on home visits, and when I climb in, I reach over and give her a kiss on the cheek. She kisses me back.

"Oh, Rachel, I'm so sorry Daddy and I were fighting at dinner, honey, I'm so sorry! And we were so worried when we realized you weren't at home. Thank you for texting me."

She reaches over and gives me a hug. I hold on tight and then I lose it. Completely lose it.

Mom wraps me in her arms and rubs my back. Of course she thinks I'm crying about her and Dad, which I am, maybe a little, but I'm mostly crying about His Creepness.

"Mom, I have to tell you—" Right then there is a knock on the window, and guess who is standing there.

Mom kisses my forehead and rolls down her window.

"Rabbi," she practically chirps. "How *nice* to *see* you."

Who the hell knocks on a closed window of a car when a kid is crying in her mother's arms? I'm beginning to think this guy has boundary issues.

"Is everything OK?" he says in that oh-so-caring tone he has.

Mom looks at me, and I shake my head slightly, meaning don't say anything to him. She gets it.

"Oh yes, Rabbi, everything is fine now," she says in her fake polite voice. Usually I hate that voice of hers, but right now I'm deeply grateful for it.

"Rachel was having kind of an off night in class," the rabbi says, and I want to kill him. Arrogant creep. Phony. Freak. But at least he is generous enough not to point out that I was not there after the break.

I put my head in my hands so I won't scream and curse or get out of the car and punch him in his stupid holier-than-thou rabbi face.

"My fault," says my mother, and no more.

"I doubt it," the rabbi says. "I can't imagine *you* doing anything wrong, Evie."

Evie?

No one calls my mother Evie except my father and my grandparents—grandmother. *Her name is Evelyn*.

"Oh, you'd be surprised," my mother says. Is she flirting with him? No. I can't process this right now.

"Well, take care, ladies. You are two of my favorite girls, you know."

Fuck you, you flirting bastard.

"Bye, Rabbi," my mother says, and then sighs.

I make myself stay quiet until I'm sure he's walked away. Then I pick up my head to tell her.

But when I see her face, I can't say a word. She's not looking at me. She's staring after the rabbi, smiling. A happy, secret—*satisfied?*—smile.

Why the hell is she smiling like that?

CHAPTER 5

DON'T LET THE GODDAMN SUN SHINE

If that was sleep, then Cheez Whiz is cheese.

Dad came into my room early, whistling as he always does, and it made me dive deeper under the covers.

Every morning of my life since I started preschool, my father has come in, opened the curtains, and pulled up the shades. My room faces east, so it is very bright and cheerful when the sun is shining. He sings, "Let the sunshine, let the sunshine in." From the musical *Hair*. Corny, yes. But it's a nice way to wake up.

Not today.

Fifteen minutes later, when my alarm goes off, I groan and hit the snooze button. I usually look forward to Thursdays because I have a great schedule (meaning study hall first thing and no math) and Yearbook after school. But today the sun shining so brightly pisses me off. Royally. The happiness of the day is wrong on so many levels.

I finally pull myself out of bed only because my bladder is ready to burst, and although I consider it, wetting the bed does not seem like the best option. As I walk to the bathroom, I get pissed off at the sun even more because it highlights every speck of dust on every surface of my room. My dresser is covered with dust, my desk is covered with dust, my floor is filthy. We have a cleaning lady who comes every other week, but Mom told her not to come in here unless I've straightened up, which I pretty much never do. With all the time I've spent in my room lately hiding from my parents' fights, you'd think I'd have gotten so bored I would have cleaned it. But no.

I pee, throw cold water on my face, put on the same clothes I was wearing yesterday (because who the eff cares), and go downstairs.

Mom has made granola. I smell it as I walk into the kitchen. She does this two or three times a year. Her granola is megagood. It *should* cheer me up. But this morning the smell of it (toasted oats, honey, vanilla, almonds, walnuts, pecans) and the look of it (all golden brown with bright red cranberries, yellow raisins, sour cherries, dried blueberries) cooling on the cookie sheets makes me madder. I do the weighing-of-the-hands thing to myself:

Mom's homemade granola vs.
the rabbi screwing someone on the *bima*.

And:

Mom's homemade granola vs.
Mom and the rabbi flirting.

Nope. Mom's granola is good, but it's not that good.

I eat some anyway, but I try very hard not to enjoy it.

To make matters weirder, now Dad's tiptoeing around me, all quiet, which is not like him. He usually chatters away about stuff in the news, what he's doing that day, the weather. He is *such* a morning person. But now he's practically silent. Mom must have just told him I bawled in the car last night.

I take a second helping of granola and sit back down. I open up my history book; I didn't read today's chapters yet. But the words are a blur, and I'm grateful when Dad says, "Hey, Raebee," and reaches his hand over to me and pats my shoulder.

"Hey, Dad," I say.

"Mom said you were upset last night. What about?"

What am I going to say? Dad, I was upset because the rabbi is a cheating liar and was screwing someone in the sanctuary and, oh, by the way, I think Mom is in love with him?

"I'm fine," I snap.

Dad doesn't say anything, just gets up and pours some more coffee for himself.

I pretend to read about New Orleans's Ninth Ward levee problem. I know I would find this interesting if I could actually tell the difference between an *a* and an *o*. But the words make no sense to me at all.

Mom walks in and makes a show of going over to Dad and giving him a big kiss. A big, long, noisy kiss on the lips. Give me a friggin' break.

I slam my book shut, take my bowl to the sink, run some water in it, and start to walk away.

Mom says, "In the dishwasher, Rachel."

I put it, and my spoon, into the dishwasher, loudly.

"Wanna ride to school, Jewel?" Dad says.

"No, I want to walk."

"Do you have *time?*" Mom asks, looking at the clock on the microwave. She knows I don't.

"I have study hall first period, and they don't care if you're late for study hall." It's a lie. I will get into trouble if I'm late, even for study hall. But I *have* to walk, have to get out of here, and now. If I walk really fast, I'll probably make it before the bell. Besides, I'm never late, and if I'm late once, I won't get in trouble, and well, really, who cares?

I get my bag and leave before they can argue. I hear them calling after me, but I ignore them.

When I walk into school, the halls are eerily quiet. Obviously, the bell has already rung.

My instinct is to run, but if I walk normally, I won't call attention to myself. So I walk as if it is the most natural thing in the world that I am the only one in the hall. One of the guidance counselors passes me, we nod, I keep walking. Being a good girl all these years just paid off.

When I get to study hall, I am ready to make my excuse (missed bus, no one could drive me), but it's a sub, and she just looks at me. So I shrug and sit down. Good.

I pull out my history book again and try to concentrate. I read the same words over and over again.

> **Hurricane Katrina was a disaster for the city of New Orleans. The floodwalls and levees that had been constructed by the U.S. Army Corps of Engineers failed to protect the city. *Designs flawed. Human***

> *error.* Nearly 80 percent of the city flooded. *Flooded. Flooded.* More than fifteen hundred people died. Some are still missing as of this writing. *Missing as of this writing. Missing. Missing. Human error. Neglect. Abuse of power. Abuse of power. Power. Abuse. Abuse.*

I feel a nudge. The kid next to me is passing a note. My name is on the front.

I open it up. It's from Jake. We have assigned seats, and he's on the opposite side of the room.

You OK? Didn't seem like yourself last night. —J.

His handwriting is neat, but not too neat. I like that.

I wish I could tell him. Last night, I thought I should tell someone, had to tell, but today I have this strong feeling that if I don't keep quiet, it will come back to bite me in the ass. As if it's my fault the rabbi seduced that girl. And my fault that I heard it.

Still, I want to answer Jake's note. What can I say to him that is not a lie but is not the whole truth either? After a long time thinking, I write,

Parents fighting at home.

Well, it's the truth. I add:

Not pretty.

Then I fold the paper back up, nowhere near as neatly as he had it folded, and send it back to him. From across the room, I watch him read it, frown, shake his head, and write something. He looks at me, our eyes meet, and he smiles. Oh. I feel better.

He starts to hand the note to the kid next to him, but the

substitute teacher clears her throat, grabs it from Jake, and throws it into the garbage can.

Oh man. I want to know what he wrote.

What difference is it to her?

I walk up to the garbage can, and as she stares at me, I take out the note.

No, I don't. But I sure think about it for the rest of study hall. Instead of reading. I'll get it on my way out.

When the bell rings, I walk in a beeline right to the garbage can. But when she sees me coming, she stands there, her arms crossed. Oh, come *on*.

I look at her, raise my eyebrows. "Please?" I whisper. But she shakes her head. I look at Jake, but he has chemistry class in the other building and has to run to make it. We wave good-bye. I look at the sub again and say, louder this time, "Please?"

She says, "No." I glare at her and then walk away, because it's not that big a deal, really, not worth getting into trouble over.

But as I walk out the door, I say "bitch" quietly, under my breath.

Immediately, I feel scared. What if she heard me? But she didn't. And besides, she can't do anything to me. She doesn't even know my name.

Next period, I am called down to the office.

Vice Principal: "Rachel, Miss Ellison says you called her a bad name."

Apparently our regular study hall teacher has our names on a seating chart. Either that or the sub is psychic.

Me (innocently): "Who is Miss Ellison?"

V.P. (eyebrows raised): "The substitute teacher you had in first-period study hall."

Me: "Oh."

V.P.: "Well?"

Me: "Why would I call her a bad name?"

Deny it without lying. How *do* I know how to do this stuff?

V.P.: "Rachel, you have never been in my office for discipline before, and I find it hard to believe you would say something like that, but she was upset and called me. So either you did or you didn't call her a bit—"

Oh, he almost said it! I frown.

V.P.: "Rachel?"

Me (sweetly): "I don't know what she's talking about."

I frown again, looking hurt. I am almost not lying.

V.P.: "OK, just—if you have her again, you might want to, uh, stay clear of her."

He believes me. Wow.

Me: "Yes, sir. Thank you."

I almost curtsy as I leave his office. Phew.

Well. For a few minutes I didn't think about my parents or the effing rabbi! Well, at least being in school is distracting.

But when I walk back into the main office, who is sitting there but Adam. He nods at me, without a smile. The usual impish sparkle is nowhere to be seen.

"Why are you here?" I ask him.

"I skipped French," he says quietly. "Got caught smoking in the bathroom." He looks—can it be?—scared.

"They called your parents?"

He nods.

"They coming in?"

He nods, then shakes his head. "Not him. Only my mom. My father—too busy, you know."

I shake my head. Right. That lying, cheating shit of a rabbi is his father. His *daddy*. For the first time ever I feel sorry for Adam.

"Why are *you* here?" he asks me.

I nod my head at the V.P., who has come out of his office and is standing behind him. Then I shake my head.

"Adam," says the V.P.

Adam stands up. "What did you *do*?" he whispers into my ear, his arm lightly around me for just a second.

"Nothing, really," I say, pulling away. He has given me the chills again.

I run down the hall and upstairs so I'm not horribly late for history class, even though I'm armed with a note from the V.P.

McKelvy tells me to hurry up and sit down. He is giving a pop quiz on last night's reading about Katrina.

I am so screwed.

CHAPTER 6

NOT LIKE A VIRGIN

I managed to answer ten questions on that quiz. There were twenty. It is the first time I have flunked anything.

When McKelvy passes the quizzes back today, confirming my fear with a big red F, I plead with him to let me make it up. He says he'll think about it. That he's a good guy, but if he makes an exception for me, yadda, yadda, yadda. Yeah, I get it.

I manage to make it through the rest of the day without walking into any walls, tripping down steps, or getting into any more trouble. I consider this a major victory. I get out early on Fridays, at one-twenty, so when I get home, no one is there except for Panda, who stretches and meows when she sees me. I grab her and retreat to my room.

I lie on my bed admiring Panda's markings as she sits on my stomach: she is so black where she is black and so white where she is white. She purrs, I chill, but my mind starts bouncing. I can't stay still anymore. I get up, holding Panda in my arms, and put her down gently on the bed. I start to pick clothes off the bed and the floor and put them away, neatly. Then I start in on the trash.

This is serious. Panda runs out.

By the time Mom and Dad get home at five o'clock, I have taken bags and bags of garbage out of my room: paper bags filled with old school papers for recycling; garbage bags of actual garbage—candy wrappers, orange peels, pieces of unidentifiable food (from the last time Alexis slept over? before the summer? that's beyond disgusting); old toys and piles of clothes and books, posters, pictures to give away.

I've put everything except the garbage down in the family room, which is where we always put stuff to donate, and I am dusting and vacuuming and Windexing like crazy while they are making dinner. Every once in a while, one of them peeks into my room.

Finally, Dad walks in, hands me a glass of water, and says, "Who are you and what have you done with my Rachel?" but then he walks back out quickly, as if to say, "I don't want to know."

By the time he comes back from picking up Grandma and the three of them come to tell me dinner is ready (I'm sure Grandma made the strenuous trip up the stairs only because she couldn't believe I had really cleaned), no one can recognize my room. Not even me. Mom and Dad are truly scared. I can see it in their eyes.

Mom says, "Shower?" and I smell my pits. She's right. I take a quick one, throw on a pair of pants I found that I had forgotten about and a T-shirt I've never worn, and go downstairs.

The dining room table is our usual Shabbat table: the white tablecloth and the good china, the silver candlesticks, the challah on the special plate given to Mom and Dad for their wedding.

I find it reassuring. Mom, Grandma, and I say the blessing over the candles, Dad says *kiddush* and *ha-motzi*, and then, as we are eating our first delicious pieces of challah pulled from the loaf, I tell them I'm not going with them to temple.

They stare at me. I quickly demolish most of the challah, scooping out the soft inside, my favorite part. They don't ask why or ask me what prompted the room cleaning or ask me how school was this week (their usual Friday night conversation).

"What?" Mom says finally. This is a bigger deal than usual. I don't go every Friday night, more like once every month or two. But tonight is a special service honoring their friends the Silversteins, who've contributed a lot of time and money to the temple. The Oneg Shabbat, the party after services, is being given by a close friend of Grandma's, Mrs. Philips, who is a fantastic baker.

I don't actually want to miss the Oneg, not that part. Mrs. Philips makes the best devil's food cake in the universe. Rich, dark chocolate. Sinful vanilla buttercream frosting between the layers and on top.

If I could get away with going only to the Oneg, I would. But I can't go to services. No way. I could not possibly sit in *that* room and listen to His Phoniness pontificate from the (I can't help but think of it this way) fucking *bima*.

"How will we explain it to the Silversteins if you're not there? It's their big night. You are so dear to them," says Mom.

Oh please. They won't even notice.

"They'll understand," I say. "I'm not feeling well."

"So if you're not feeling well, I guess you won't be going out at all this weekend?"

Touché, Mama Bear.

"I mean emotionally," I say. "Not physically." This is, of course, true.

"Well then, a little sanctuary time is in order, wouldn't you agree?" she says.

Sanctuary time? Is that what they call it now? If she only knew.

I look at Grandma. She used to be my shopping buddy, my chick-flick-watching partner, my ally, the one who took my side in fights with Mom. But ever since Grandpa died, she's been a shadow of her former self. She is picking at her noodle *kugel*, not looking up at all. I'm not even sure she's paying attention.

"Grandma, help," I say, but she keeps picking.

I give my father a pleading look. Dad, who I swear only goes to temple to please Mom, shakes his head slightly. "Sorry, Rae-bee, I gotta go with Mom here. I think you should come."

She smiles at him, he smiles at her, and then it's as if they're alone in the room. What is it with them? This hot-and-cold thing is driving me crazy.

"I hate you," I say, and I storm up to my room, or to what used to be my room.

My phone vibrates. A text. It's Adam.

`Gotta go to temple 2nite. Pls come.`

Huh. I text back:

`Punishment?`

`Yup. But u being there will make it OK.`

Hmmmm. Adam wants *me* to come? I text him back, my heart beating a little faster than I would like.

OK

I take off my pants and top, throw them onto the floor, and go stand in my closet.

What to wear? Something the parental police will think is appropriate but that is not too uncool. A black skirt, red tank top, black sweater over that. Black leggings, black ballet slippers. I throw on my coat before they can tell me to button up the sweater.

I get a lecture in the car about not saying the word *hate*, but they don't put a lot of oomph into it. I should be happy about that, but for some reason I'm not.

When I walk into the sanctuary, I swear I get post-traumatic stress syndrome. Seeing the dark blue velvet cushions and the blond wood, smelling that musty-old-prayer-book-ladies-in-perfume-old-man-onion-sweet-wine-so-many-people smell—brings it all back. I can't even look at the *bima*. I turn around to leave and bump smack into Alexis.

"What are you doing here?" I ask her. She hasn't been to services in forever.

But there's Adam, next to her. Alexis raises her fingers to her lips as if she's holding a joint and sucks in. "Wanna meet us out back during the sermon? You'll enjoy the Oneg much more."

"Come on, Rachel, time to lose your virginity," says Adam, and he raises his eyebrows. Acting like he didn't text me. "I mean your pot virginity, Rachel," and he and Alexis both laugh. I *did* try pot once, at camp, but nothing happened. I guess Alexis forgot I told her that. I *am* curious to try again, but at temple? Really? And then Adam leans in close to me and whispers in my ear (why does he keep doing that?), "We can always take care of the other kind when we're alone." Chills again. *Damn* him.

Alexis, Adam, and I are blocking the doorway of the sanctuary, so everyone has to walk around us going in. I am about to move away when Jake comes toward me.

"Hi, Rachel," he says, looking into my eyes. We haven't talked since study hall. His eyes lock with mine, and they're so penetrating I lose my balance and step back right into some lady who snaps, "Careful!"

These boys are driving me crazy.

"Sorry," I say, grabbing on to Jake's arm.

"Hey, hey," says Dr. Schmidt, Jake's dad, who's the new president of the synagogue. "You kids are in the way." He's smiling at us, though.

"Sorry, Dad," says Jake.

"Sorry," I mumble again. Adam and Alexis have disappeared.

"Please go sit down, son," he says, patting Jake on the back. Jake looks at me, but I smile, shrug, point vaguely in the other direction, and turn around.

No way am I going in there.

I walk quickly down the hall to my favorite bathroom. No one is in here, but there are a bunch of girls' coats thrown on the couch. I burrow under them and go to sleep.

I don't know how long I've been hibernating under the coats, but I wake up to a giggle of little girls walking in.

It must be sermon time.

I sit up and climb out from the pile. The girls squeal and scream.

"Grrrr," I say, making a monster face, my hands up in the air, like claws. "Grrr . . ."

More squeals, and laughter, as they pile onto the couch in a puppy heap.

I go to the parking lot out back.

CHAPTER 6A

NOT A VIRGIN

Adam and Alexis are definitely high. They are giggling and telling stupid jokes as we walk back into the temple. I feel nothing.

With my first toke I had a coughing fit. That didn't happen at camp, but I don't think I was doing it right then. This time I inhaled big and it really hurt going in, but they said it would be easier the second time. They told me how to inhale, how to hold it in. It didn't hurt the second time, but I don't think I did it right, because I feel nothing. So they kept getting me to take more hits, as they called them. Why are they called hits? Or tokes? Why not just puffs? Or drags? It did get easier and easier to do the whatever-you-want-to-call-thems. You? Who's you? Who am I talking to?

When I said I wasn't stoned, Adam said he didn't feel anything his first time either. I said it wasn't my first time, but Alexis interrupted me, saying she had felt something *her* first time. I think she was lying to impress Adam. She would do that. But I could tell. Couldn't he? Not if he's stoned, I guess. I'm not stoned. I wish I were. Stoned, I mean, not lying. Stoned. Wish I were.

Wish, witch, which. Which way did Adam and Alexis go? Where are they? Should I walk into the temple? How should I walk into the temple? Through the kitchen? Or should I go around to the front? Where are they? Oh, there they are, in front of me, walking down the ramp from the parking lot, in through the kitchen. I remember one time cooking pancakes in that kitchen with Dad. That was nice. We had to make, like, four hundred pancakes for a Brotherhood breakfast. Pancakes. Oooh. Pancakes would taste pretty good right now. Or waffles. I like waffles better. All those nooks and crannies for the maple syrup to get stuck in.

I wish it had worked. I wish I were stoned. Maybe I wouldn't feel so horrible. All I feel is let down. I wish I were stoned.

I'd better go in. Oh, I am in. How did I get here? I'm here in the auditorium. It's like I'm not in me, I'm outside me looking at me. I felt this way the other night, in class after—God. Oh God. Oh no, don't go there, Rachel. Look. Look around you. Look at all the people in here.

Wow. *Look* at all these people. How will I ever get through them to the devil's food cake?

How long have I been standing here looking at the crowd? I think I've been standing here for a long time. I should go get some of the devil's food cake. It's going to taste soooo good.

Oh man, there it is. I am going to stuff two pieces in my mouth. Oh God. I stuff in a third. It tastes soooo good.

CHAPTER 7

DEVIL'S FOOD CAKE 'N' COFFEE MAN, MAN

Do I have frosting all over my face? Did I really have five pieces? Am I going to regret this tomorrow? I am *so* going to regret this tomorrow.

But it doesn't matter . . . Alexis and Adam and I are having so much fun. I love Alexis! She's whispering to Adam. He's whispering back.

Wait. Are they whispering about me? Nah. They're probably whispering about everyone else in the room, right? All the kids who didn't go out back with us, the old people who are acting like it's a regular Oneg. I mean, why would they be whispering about me? But why are they looking at me?

"Hey, guys," I say.

They look up, deer in headlights.

"Shit, are you whispering about me?"

Alexis shakes her head in slow motion. Adam shakes his head, shrugs his shoulders, bursts out laughing. Cookie crumbs spray out of his mouth, which makes Alexis laugh hysterically, and now Mrs. Rabbi is walking over to us.

Oh, I should tell her! I should tell her right now. Mrs. Rabbi—I mean, Mrs. Cohn, I heard your husband in the sanctuary. He was screwing this bride chick.

"Adam, kids, what are you *doing*?" she says through gritted teeth. I've never actually seen someone talk like that. It's kind of a miracle. Her teeth are clenched, but words are coming out.

I'm going to try it. I clench. I will tell her about her husband through gritted teeth.

Making noises but no real words. It's too hard. How do you actually form words?

She is looking at me with a very weird expression.

Did she understand what I was saying? Was I even talking?

I feel a hand on me, a tug, pulling me away from Mrs. Rabbi.

I turn around and it's Jake.

Jake!

Ah, Jake. Jake, who was my friend in kindergarten and then moved away for so many years. And now he's back. With his beautiful back.

Hee. Jake.

He looks at me looking at him. He doesn't say anything. I smile at him. I think. I hope I'm smiling.

His eyes are so sexy. He's kind of a nerd but he has sexy eyes. Can you be a nerd with sexy eyes? Can you be a nerd *and* a jock? Can you be a nerd jock with sexy eyes and a back that women would jump through hoops for? Get it? Jump through hoops for? I'm cracking myself up.

"You think I'm a nerd?" he says.

I have GOT to stop thinking out loud.

"No. Yes. But I also think you have sexy eyes and a strong back," I say.

Pot = truth serum.

I smile my most winning smile and try to talk my way out of this: "You are an enigma. A paradox. A mystery to me."

"And *you* are a girl whose beautiful face is covered with cake and icing," Jake says, taking a napkin and wiping off my face.

Did he call me beautiful?

"Thanks," I say, and I feel really stupid. Does he know I'm stoned? Am I stoned? I am sooooo stoned.

"It's pretty stupid to get stoned at temple," he whispers.

"I'm not stoned," I say.

"Shhhh, you're shouting," Jake says, nodding his head. Two old ladies are staring at me. Oh shit, one of them is Mrs. Silverstein. I wave at her and smile. "*Mazel tov!*" I mouth.

"I thought the pot hadn't worked," I whisper to Jake.

"Oh, it worked," he says, and he takes me by the arm and leads me to some chairs under the windows on the far side of the auditorium, far away from all the people—and the food.

"What if I want more food?" I whine to him as he gently makes me sit down.

"I'll get it for you. I'll also get you coffee."

"Does that help?"

Jake shrugs. "Never tried it."

"Pot or coffee?"

"Wouldn't you like to know?" he says, and smiles.

"You have a sexy smile, too, and I know I said that out loud."

"You are so going to regret this in the morning," he says. "But I'm not." He holds up his phone.

"You're recording this?"

"Just that last part," he says, and tucks his phone into his front pants pocket. I reach into his pocket, feel around.

Jake pulls my hand out. "Rachel," he says. "Seriously." He's blushing.

I am so ashamed. But I'm not the one who should feel ashamed. The stupid rabbi should feel ashamed.

"What?" asks Jake. "Why should the rabbi feel ashamed?"

"Did I say that?"

Jake nods.

Oh shit. My heart starts beating wildly. I think I'm going to have a heart attack.

"Jake," I whisper frantically into his ear, "was I talking when you pulled me away before? Away from Mrs. Cohn? Was I saying something out loud?"

If my life were a movie, it would be called *Rachel and the Temple of Doom*.

"No, I don't think so. I didn't hear anything. I think you were just staring at her."

"How long were you standing there?"

"Long enough."

"Oh, thank God." Maybe there *is* a God! And He/She is looking out for me! I feel so happy all of a sudden. Happy, happy, happy. And strong and relieved and powerful and—

"How about we go back to me telling you that you're sexy? Get out the phone," I say in my sexiest voice.

"Are you kidding? I'm not falling for that. You're going to grab it from me and erase what I recorded. You may be stoned, but you're not stupid."

I nod again. I am very stoned. I feel like I might start to cry. "Please, Jake," I whisper. "Help me."

"Don't move," he says, and runs his fingers gently through my hair as he pushes it back off my face. "Do not go anywhere or talk to anyone. I am getting you some coffee."

I sit and wait for Jake. I love him. I pledge myself to him forever. But it is taking him so long to get my coffee. Why does it take four hours to get coffee?

"It took me three minutes," he says, shaking his head sadly. "You are really gone. I am going to kill Adam."

"It's not Adam's fault. Besides, it was Alexis's stuff."

"Huh," he says, and he hands me the coffee. "I put lots of sugar in it. And cream. Drink up."

The coffee tastes delicious going down, but I'm afraid now I am just going to be a highly caffeinated stoned person.

"I bet there's a market for this," I say. "Coffee with pot. Get it? Coffee pot!" I am so funny. I'm usually funny, but when I'm stoned I'm a riot.

"You're funnier when you're straight," Jake says.

He gets me another cup, makes me drink it, and then insists we take a walk outside. As we leave the auditorium, I see my mother smiling at me with approval. She likes Jake. I won't let that bother me. I like him, too.

"You're my savior," I tell him.

"I am not your savior," he says. "I'm merely your coffee man. For tonight . . ."

I don't know what he means. I don't want to know what he means. I'm never having sex, never having a boyfriend. Not after that stupid rabbi . . .

I am sad. I whimper, whine. Very attractive, Rachel.

"Hang in there, Rachel," Jake says. "You'll feel better when we get outside."

He steers me out the front of the building.

When the cool air hits me, I laugh. "Oh, that *does* feel good!"

"I'm so glad!" Jake laughs too. "Let's walk." He holds my arm as we go down the steps. They are very steep, these steps. I never realized that.

"Can we get on flat land?" I ask him.

"We'll walk around the block, silly, stoned Rachel."

I know this block so well, but in my current state I am seeing all kinds of things I never saw before. Trees that need to be touched. How can bark be rough and smooth at the same time? A window that has to be looked into. An ordinary family watching TV. How nice. Steps to a house that have to be climbed up and down a few times, with Jake holding my arm.

Jake talks, and keeps talking, about school, about swimming, how he sometimes thinks about trying to go to the Olympics, but he doesn't think he's good enough. I want to ask him more about that, but it will have to wait until I can actually form sentences from complicated thoughts. Or at least complete thoughts.

"I don't like feeling this way," I say. "What if someone knows? What if I get arrested?"

"Shhhh, shhhh," Jake says. "I'll protect you."

After a few minutes, or years, a few times around the block, I feel less panicked. And "I need some more cake!"

Jake reaches into his pocket and says, "Ta-da!" He pulls out a chocolate chip cookie.

"Aw," I say. "I want the devil's food cake."

"The icing in my pocket, not so good," Jake says, and I don't know why, but I reach up and kiss him on the cheek.

"That doesn't count as our first kiss," he says, handing me the cookie.

"It isn't our first kiss!" I say.

"Huh?"

"Don't you remember?" I feel so sad that he doesn't remember. Dejected. Rejected. Ejected. "*Don't* you?"

He looks at me with a question in those intense eyes.

"In the kindergarten block corner. Remember?" I say. "I was wearing a cowboy hat and spurs. You were wearing a pink gown and pearls?"

Jake laughs. "That was *you*?"

"Yes that was *me*!" Angrily I pull away from him and walk quickly by myself, chomping on the cookie.

Ouch! That bump in the sidewalk got bigger since the last time we went by. Jake picks me up and puts his arm around me, holding me tight.

"I remembered," he says. "I was just trying to be, I don't know, cool. But of course I remember."

I look at him. "And then you moved away," I say. "Why did you move away?"

"My dad had to go for his residency. We were supposed to move right back when he was done, but then . . ." Jake stops and looks at me, shakes his head. His eyes are really so beautiful. And sad. Why are they sad?

"What?" I say.

He shakes his head again and then looks like he's going to say something, and for some stupid reason I start to giggle. The whole situation strikes me as very funny, but I couldn't say why.

"Never mind," Jake says. "Let's keep walking." And so we walk, and we talk about nothing much, but his eyes stay sad, and even in my stoned state I know something just happened, but I have no idea what.

By the time my mother calls me to say it is time to go home, I am still stoned, but I know to keep quiet.

She and Dad pull up beside us, and Jake helps me get into the backseat of the car. Grandma's not here. Must have gotten a ride home with someone else. Before he closes the door, he bends his head toward me, and I reach up my hand to touch him, his face, his slightly too long brown hair. I want to run my fingers through the waves—why didn't I do that on our walk?—but I can't quite reach, and he doesn't bend any farther. Instead he stands up, gives me a nod and a little smile. I mouth, "Thank you," and give him a big smile. His grin expands to fill his whole face.

I don't say a word to my parents, partly to hang on to that moment, partly in self-preservation. They don't talk either.

When we get home, I mutter, "Good night," go right up to my room, which is too neat to look like my room, and fall onto the bed and into a dream-filled, fitful sleep. I dream of devil's food cake and Jake and Adam and Alexis. I wake up with a start, heart pounding, don't know why.

It's three in the morning. I am *parched*.

In the kitchen I drink a glass of orange juice and a gallon of ice water. On my way back upstairs I hear rustling in the living room. Dad's sleeping on the couch again.

CHAPTER 8

THE MORNING AFTER

I think I have a pot hangover. And I'm stuck on the pot. Which makes me a captive audience to Mom and Dad's fight downstairs.

Now I know what is meant by "the morning after." I don't ever want to do *that* again. I'm not sure what I mean by *that*—getting stoned or eating enough sugar to fuel a third-world nation. That nation being an angry and hungry one whose army is, at the moment, fighting my intestines—and winning, hands down. Or butt down, really.

If I ever get out of this bathroom, I'm going to go online and make a significant contribution to our armed forces.

Do they think I can't hear them? And of course, to completely drive me mad, I hear only some sentences—the ones that are really screamed.

Dad: "I know you never really loved me! I know you think you settled!"

Can't hear anything for a few minutes.

Mom: "How do you know anything? You never LISTEN to me!"

Dad: "All I DO is listen to you! You never let me get a word in edgewise!"

Could this be any dumber? It's like they're reading a movie script of a fight!

Dad again: "You wish you had married that other guy, don't you? Steve whatshisname?"

Holy crap. What's that about?

Mom: "What are you TALKING about?"

Dad: "I can tell you're not here with me so much of the time. You're somewhere else. Are you in touch with him, Evie? Is that what you're doing every night, talking to him?"

Not Steve Somebody, Dad, I want to shout, it's the *rabbi*! But no, I don't know that. I don't. It can't be.

I don't hear anything for a long, long time.

Then my dad's voice, sad, soft, but loud enough for me to hear, which means they're standing at the bottom of the steps by the front door. "I don't know what to do. What to say to you. I just don't."

"I know you don't," says my mother loudly. "And that's the whole problem."

Slammed door.

"Shit!" says my dad.

Another slammed door.

Car engine.

Another car engine.

I poop my guts out for a few more minutes and finally get up. I look out the window. Both cars *are* gone.

Not my parents. Please not *my* parents.

• • •

Two hours later and nobody has come back. I have to get out. My bowels have calmed down, so I text Alexis.

I need perspective. Maybe she can give me some. Because of her brothers, she's always seemed older than me. That used to be a good thing. She was generous with her wisdom. It was one of the best things about her. Is. Still. I hope. Maybe she'll come through for me. At least we could laugh.

She texts me right back.

`Yes.`

Yes!

I get on Sir Walter and pedal with more energy and optimism than I've had since "Oh, Rabbi." I love fall, the colored leaves, the crisp, cool air. I tilt my face to the sun.

And yet . . . I probably shouldn't have my hopes up. But I do. I did say I'd treat her to a coffee, but still . . .

When I get to the Starbucks by the Acme, I worry by the way she's standing there that she's got her wall up. I smile anyway. She says she'll find a table while I get the drinks. I consider bolting, but I don't.

"Took you long enough," she says when I sit down with my peppermint tea and her latte. I bristle. It was *her* drink that took so long—and, by the way, was more expensive. But I decide to woo her instead of getting mad.

"What, the people-watching wasn't any good?" I say. "Girl in the corner, purple shirt."

She looks at me, smiles. Our old game.

"Thirty seconds, go!" I say.

She studies the girl, turns back to me, grins. "Eighth grade. Cheerleading reject, joined Pep Squad instead. Will be a pom-pom girl in high school."

"Excellent," I say.

"OK. Yours," Alexis says. "Boy in checked shirt two tables over. Thirty seconds, go!"

He looks a lot like Kenny, the genius in my math class, but a few years older. I got this. "OK, this guy is . . . a freshman at the college. Lives at home, saving money to get out as soon as possible. Chemistry major. Parents want him to be a research scientist. He wants to be a—hmmm—psychologist. Never been laid." I look at him more closely; he is *built*. "Plays tennis."

Alexis looks him over. "Good one! I wouldn't have guessed psychologist, but I think you're right! Name?"

Hmmm. He's Asian, but born here, I'm sure. "Daniel—no, Brandon. No. Branden with an *e*."

"Yes!"

"And what's your girl's name?"

Alexis looks long and hard. "Could be Jenna, or Madison. No. I've got it!" she says, the old Alexis smile lighting up her face. "Tiffany. Definitely Tiffany."

"Definitely!"

And then we both say, at exactly the same time, "Tiffany Dawn!"

We smile at each other. Maybe even beam.

Alexis.

She takes a gulp of her latte; I sip my tea.

"Thanks so much for coming," I say.

"So what's up?" she says with a small yawn.

"Rough night?" I say, smiling. "I had a rough morning. Too much cake!"

She shrugs. Uh-oh. I'm losing her. Is she pissed off I got stoned with her and Adam? Does she want him all to herself?

"I don't *like* Adam, you know," I tell her.

"What?" she says. "Oh, neither do I. I'm still hung up on my boyfriend in California." She runs her fingers through her short hair. I'm getting used to it. I think. But how weird is it that I don't even know her boyfriend's name?

"Alexis, tell me his name, for God's sake! What *is* it?"

"Mitch."

I nod.

"I nicknamed him Mustache, because he grew one for a couple of days, but it looked dorky so he shaved it. I still call him that just to annoy him."

"Funny," I say, not with a lot of conviction.

"Look," she says, "I think Branden with an *e* is checking out Tiffany Dawn!"

We both look at him.

"Go for it, Branden," I say loudly. He turns and looks at me. Do I know you? his look says.

"Oh my God!" Alexis says. "Brilliant! You are so brilliant!" and we break into peals of laughter.

Branden looks at us, wondering, then goes back to his work. It's a first. Neither of us has ever guessed a name right—that we know, of course.

Alexis is smiling at me as she sips her coffee.

"So listen," I say, grabbing the moment. "I, uh, have to tell you something."

She straightens her back, narrows her eyes, looks away from me. Her guard is up. Why?

I whisper across the table, "It's about . . . the rabbi, the other night. In the sanctuary. I heard noises."

"When, last night?"

I shake my head. "Last week, before confirmation class."

She looks at me blankly. I don't want to say the words I have to say to get it across to her. But what's the big deal? Why do I care so much? So I just say it. "I heard the rabbi, with a woman, you know, in the sanctuary. Doing it. I think."

Alexis smirks.

"I'm not kidding," I say. "I'm not making a joke."

"So you heard the rabbi fucking someone?"

I nod my head vigorously. "On the *BIMA*!" I say. "Can you believe it?"

"Big whoop," she says, fiddles with a sugar packet. Yawns again. But I know I see a look in her eyes: shock, disappointment.

"It wasn't his wife," I say. "It was the *rabbi*. Rabbi Cohn. With some—some girl. A bride, I think."

"So?" She sips her coffee.

I stare at her. "What do you mean, so? Isn't that awful? The rabbi was doing it, the RABBI!"

"Big fucking deal, Rachel. Why do you care so much? He's just a guy, a man, Rachel. Hairy legs and a penis. Blood, guts, shit. He's not God, you know."

"But—"

She shakes her head, and I hear her mutter something, something that sounds like "Stupid, perfect Rachel." But that can't be what she said.

"What was that?" I ask her.

She shrugs.

"Alexis! What. Did. You. Say?"

"Rachel, just because you have this perfect little life, with these perfect parents, it doesn't mean that everyone else does, you know. Grow the hell up."

"But, Alexis—"

"You are such a *baby*," she says.

I am not. That's what I want to say. To scream. But I don't. I'm too busy trying not to cry. Like a baby.

Now I play with the sugar and sweetener packets too. Try to make a house, but it keeps falling down.

"Alexis," I finally manage, "my life is *not* perfect, my parents are not perfect. They're fighting all the time lately. It's horrible, and now the rabbi and—" I look at her, my eyes filling up, spilling over.

Her eyes meet mine for a nanosecond and then shift past me, toward the windows. She takes a long gulp of her latte, looks down at her phone. Shakes her head slightly.

"Alexis?" I say softly. "I'm really upset. I really need to talk."

She looks at me, her eyes hard.

"You weren't there for me when my parents were splitting up."

"What? You never told me. I would have been there for you, Lex, I would have!" Of course I would have. "And I'm here for you now. I know it's still hard for you. Please. Let's talk now. About everything."

She looks past me again.

"Alexis, I'm here," I say. "I care. I want us to be good again."

I feel an ocean rise between us. The roar of the ocean almost drowns out her voice. But not quite. I hear her very clearly when she finally speaks. And what she says is:

"Oh."

And then she starts texting someone.

CHAPTER 9

KISSING ELEPHANTS

I am bereft. I am furious. Furious, bereft. Back and forth. All Saturday night I think about calling her, but I don't. I am too raw; I've got nothing left. So I do homework. There *is* nothing left to do with the weekend but that.

I get my work done—math, history, English, all of it.

Monday morning she's not in school. Good. Fine.

By history class I'm feeling good enough—about school, anyway—to ask McKelvy if he's thought about whether I could take the quiz about Katrina again. He tells me to come to his classroom after school, and when I do, he makes me a proposition.

"Fine," I say to him after hearing him out. "I'm happy to do that."

He has agreed to let me take the quiz over if I go to an elementary school in the poor part of town and tutor a kid once a week. It seems like a big price to pay, but helping to save the world will do me good, I'm sure. *Tikkun olam*. One of the rabbi's things. Damn him.

"Good. I was going to ask you anyway, before the whole flunking thing," he tells me. "You'll be great at it."

"Got me," I say, but really I'm pleased. It's nice to know that someone has faith in me. And it's not just anyone, it's McKelvy.

I practically skip down the empty hall. The bell rang a long time ago, and all the buses are gone. I am looking forward to the walk home. And then—there's Jake!

He hasn't texted or called me since Friday night, and we didn't talk in school at all today.

I have decided that he thinks I'm a stoner, a loser.

But he gives me a big smile, and so I say "hi" with a big smile back.

"Why are you here so late?" he asks.

"I had to talk to McKelvy."

"Why?"

"He wants me to volunteer at Union Elementary. In their reading program."

"Cool," he says.

I should thank him for Friday night, but I'm too embarrassed. "Why are you still here?" I ask instead.

"I had to get permission from all my teachers to be out Wednesday, Thursday, and Friday for the state swim meet. They all gave me permission—*and* homework."

"So you really *are* good at swimming!"

He smiles. "You remember."

"What?"

"You remember what I told you, even though you were so stoned."

I stop, look at him seriously. "Of course I remember. I remember everything you said." And I wonder about what you didn't say, I want to add. But I don't.

Jake smiles. "I *am* good—at swimming, I mean. I should be—I've been swimming since I was about six. But I don't think I'm Olympics good. It's just that I've spent so much time in the water, I'm practically a fish."

"What kind?" I say.

"What kind of fish?"

I nod. "Yeah, if you were a fish, what kind of fish would you be?"

"Can I be a mammal who swims?" As if I had asked him the most normal question in the world.

"Sure," I say.

"A dolphin."

"Is that because you like dolphins or because you feel you *are* a dolphin? It has to be because you feel you *are* a dolphin."

He looks at me with those eyes of his. Sometimes they look hazel, sometimes brown. Right now hazel.

"I feel like a dolphin," he says. "I *am* a dolphin."

We are stopped, I realize, in the middle of the street in front of school. I realize this only because a horn honks. At us.

"Let's not have you be a dead dolphin," I say, and I grab his hand and lead him to the other side of the street. I start to pull my hand away, but he won't let me.

So we walk for a while holding hands. It's awkward because my messenger bag has slid off and down to that elbow and keeps bumping into my leg with a *thwack*. I try not to care. Step, *thwack*, step, *thwack*, step . . .

"What about you? If you were an animal, what would you be?" he asks me.

I should know the answer to this question right away. Alexis's older brothers used to ask us this stuff all the time—"If you were a store, what kind of store would you be?" and "If you could fly or make yourself invisible, which would you choose?" and, even weirder, "Gerbils for hands or pretzels for hands?"

But I can't answer Jake's question right away. I used to always say golden retriever. A happy, tail-wagging, life-is-great creature. Not so much anymore. . . .

Maybe a cat? Like Panda? She can be cuddly and friendly, or she can be aloof and strange . . . but it's always on her terms. She has a real mind of her own and—

No, that's not me, either. Panda has *kavanah*. Cat *kavanah*. She's all about *intention*. I can't find my *kavanah* anywhere lately. (Even though I cleaned up my room. Ha.)

I'm more like a bird or an insect that's caught on a breeze.

I say this aloud to Jake, and he looks confused.

"Or like a firefly that has been put in a jar without enough airholes."

Out of nowhere a biblical image comes to me: Abraham and Isaac on the mountain; I am Isaac, tied up like a ram. "Or a ram, a sacrificial ram!" I shout gleefully.

OK, now Jake's looking at me with fear and pity. And worry. This is not how I want this to be going.

Pity ≠ attraction.

"I'm just *kidding*," I say. I think for a minute and say the first thing that comes into my mind next. "Elephant." I'm immediately sorry. Elephants are big, and fat. With wrinkly skin. Definitely not sexy.

But Jake nods. "An elephant is smart, strong, empathic, nurturing. . . ." He takes his hand away from mine, fixes my messenger bag so it is on my shoulder. As he's doing it, he pushes my hair away from my face and gives me one of his long, intense looks. I think he is going to kiss me, but then he turns away and takes my hand again. We start walking together, hand in hand, not talking.

I love his hand. Strong. Dry. Not sweaty.

"Um. Rachel?"

"Yeah?"

"The thing is, you don't look like an elephant. You look more like a tiger, sleek and stunning—"

Me? Sleek and stunning?

"—or a beautiful bird, a bluebird or . . ." Jake laughs. "OK, that was really lame."

Not lame, not lame. Nice, niiiiice.

"OK. Um. What I want to say is . . ."

He stops, turns me toward him. He looks me straight in the eyes for a minute or more, without saying anything.

My heart is pounding so hard, I think I can hear it.

"You are so beautiful," Jake says.

His voice is husky, and I know where this is going, so I say stupidly, "No, no, I'm not, my hair is a mess and—"

He puts his hand to my lips, then moves it away, swings his messenger bag back so it's not between us, comes closer to me, pushes my hair away from my face again, and then puts his lips on mine.

It's a short kiss, just a peck really, and I'm disappointed when he pulls back.

But his eyes are asking, Is it OK?

I lean into him and kiss him, a little harder and a little longer than he kissed me. His lips are soft, full, wonderful.

Now I pull away and look at him. I give him a smile that I think is sexy, because I feel sexy, and

he kisses me, really kisses me, and

I really kiss him back and

I can't say anything else because that's all there is, just the two of us kissing and kissing, and everything else blissfully disappears.

CHAPTER 10
SLOPPY

When Jake and I finally part, and he goes his way and I go mine, I skip all the way home. Literally skip, like a little kid, even though I don't want to get there too fast. I can't help it. If I could fly, I would.

Yes! There are no cars in the driveway. I'll have the house to myself to luxuriate. And that is exactly what I do: I luxuriate in the memory of our kisses, walking from room to room, listening to love songs on my iPod. I play Ingrid Michaelson's "The Way I Am" twice. It's a prayer: take me the way I am.

In the old days I would have called Alexis, and I consider it for a minute, but no—no way. . . .

Instead I open the fridge, look at the jar of peanut butter, the stash of chocolate on the door. Tempting. I am hungry. But I don't want to wipe away the taste of Jake's mouth. So I plop on the living room couch and listen to my music. Panda finds me, jumps on my chest, and licks my chin. I pet her until she settles herself on my belly, purring. She warms me, and the two of us fall asleep until the door opens.

"Rachel? You home?" It's Dad. I keep my eyes closed, pretend not to hear him. He goes down to his lair in the basement, and then Mom comes home a few minutes later. She immediately starts grousing about my shoes and backpack by the kitchen door.

"Rachel, why do you need to leave a mess wherever you go? Pick up this stuff, will you?"

Panda, disloyal cat, jumps off me to go say hello to Mom, and I crank up the music so I don't have to listen to Mom, though of course I can still hear her.

"Why am I the only one who does anything around here? Dan, did you get milk like you were supposed to? Dan, where the hell are you?"

Just then someone sings in my ear, "And the walls came down, all the way to hell. . . ." I swear my iPod has an evil genius inside of it.

Jake is at my locker when I get there the next morning. Waiting for me! He's smiling.

"Hey," he says.

"Hey."

"Sorry I'm not going to be around the rest of the week."

"Me too!" I say, maybe a little too loudly. The kid who has the locker next to me, some girl on the field hockey team who never, ever acknowledges my existence, turns and looks.

"I'll try to call you from the swim meet, but I get pretty obsessed."

"Can you text?"

"Maybe. Actually, I'll be trying really hard *not* to think about you."

I am taken aback, but he is grinning so widely that I laugh. "OK . . . ," I say.

"Can't afford to get distracted." Now he's not smiling. He's looking at me with those eyes. We lean into each other, but the bell rings.

The damn bell rings.

We say a quick "bye," and every cell of my body wants to follow every cell in his body, but I take a deep breath and turn away.

It takes me a couple of minutes into bio to turn down my heat. It's not easy, because the teacher's talking about birds mating. When I see Jake later, in English class, he's on the other side of the room. I get through math, history, phys ed, hoping to see him at the end of the day at my locker, but he isn't there. I run and just make the bus.

The sight of Adam sitting in the center backseat, in his black jeans and black sneakers and maroon hoodie, with a space beside him, cheers me up a little bit. He's not Jake, but . . . he's decent company when he's alone. Alexis isn't with him. None of his pack of boys either. I nod to him, and he nods to me, pats the seat next to him.

"What's shakin', Sugarbee?"

"My head," I say, shaking it.

"Hey, what happened to your curls, Rachel? You used to have such great curly hair."

"I blow it out." Been doing it for, like, two years, and he's noticing now?

"Why do you blow it?"

"It looks better this way," I say petulantly.

"Well, you is WRONG, honey, wrong, wrong, WRONG."

He says it with the confidence of a handsome boy. A handsome boy who doesn't have to do anything but *be* to be handsome.

I shrug. I want to believe him. Think how much time I'd save if I didn't blow-dry my hair. Does Jake even know that my hair is naturally curly? Much curlier than this?

"Where were you just now? What were you thinking about?" he asks.

Jake, I want to say, but instead I say, "Nothing," and immediately feel guilty, as if I'm betraying Jake.

"You could go somewhere with *me*," he says, whispering into my ear. He takes a strand of my hair and twists it, curls it around his finger. This feels too good.

"Sorry, I've already got a ticket somewhere else."

"Oh, that hurts!" Adam says, pulling away and making a motion as if to stab himself in the heart. "You're cruel, Rachel G." But he is grinning that half grin of his, as if to say, It's OK, I'm not going to take it seriously one way or the other.

He's basically a good guy, I think.

But then of course he proves inheritance through nature or nurture and says, "I hope it's a good ride, babe," and he does that pumping thing with his hips and arms. "A goooood ride."

"Ew."

"Ride him, cowgirl!" And now he's really going at it.

"Oh, Adam, stop!" I say, and I pull out my book, put my earphones in, and turn away from him.

Adam's apple did not fall far from the tree.

When I get home, there's an email from Jake.

```
Had to run, sorry. My mom picked me up so
I could pack. The bus leaves for Harrisburg
at 5:00. I will see you when I get back. I
will not think about you. I will not think
about you. I will not.
Jake.
```

I print out his email and put it under my pillow. Am I a goner or what?

On Wednesday school sucks. No prospects of seeing Jake. Morning goes by so slowly and now at lunch it's weirder than ever with Alexis. We're still sitting at the same table we always sit at with our circle of friendlets. In the old days she and I would talk all through lunch. Now it's just silence while the others yak around us. Marissa from temple and her best friend, Kendra, are giggling about a TV show they watch.

Oh well. I don't need to talk.

I can just eat.

I take a huge bite of my sloppy joe, squeezing the roll without thinking—I mean, how stupid is that? Every kid learns by first grade not to squeeze the sloppy joe roll! And all the goop starts cascading down my—of course, to make it as awful as it can possibly be—brand-new pale blue top.

"Oh fuck," I say, jumping up and dropping the rest of the sloppy joe on my lap.

"Oh double and triple fuck!" I shout loud enough, apparently, for Mrs. Thomas, my sweet English teacher, to hear, because she comes marching at me, wagging her finger. "RayCHUL!"

Meanwhile, Kendra has come around from her side of the table with a napkin and Marissa has run off, saying, "I'll get more."

"Rachel Greenberg," Mrs. Thomas yells, "watch your mouth! I am going to have to—" But as her eyes move up and down my patheticness, she stops and says quietly, "Get yourself cleaned up, dear. And next time try to be more careful. . . ."

Next time? As much as I love them, I am never going to eat sloppy joes again.

Alexis has not said a word or moved a muscle, even though she is sitting right next to me. But when Marissa comes running back with the napkins, saying, "I wet some of them," Alexis finally turns around, takes one look at me, says, "Oh, RAY-CHUL!" and starts laughing hysterically.

Soon the whole table is laughing, even Marissa and Kendra.

I walk out of the cafeteria holding my messenger bag over myself and run to the nearest bathroom.

Me: Mom, can you please bring me a change of clothes?

Mom: I'm on my way to visit a family!

Me: Mom, I'm a mess.

Mom: Rachel, I—

Me (unable to stop myself): Waaaaaaaa.

Mom: I'll get there as soon as I can.

Me: I love you.

Of course I have math next and it starts in five minutes. I am going to get in too much trouble if I skip it, so I dry my face and do the best I can with the mess that is my shirt and pants, using a gazillion paper towels.

Luckily, Mean Math Teacher has eyes, if no heart, and when I show him my clothes and tell him my mother is coming, all he says is "Change quickly when she gets here."

I nod and walk to my desk.

Kendra and Marissa are in this class, and they come over to me and ask if I'm OK. I shrug.

The call comes right after Mean Math Teacher tells us to start on tomorrow's homework. When I walk into the office to get my clothes, there's Adam again.

"What did you do now?" I say meanly. I'm still mad at him for the pumping hips.

"Nothing. I have a 'follow-up' meeting with His Highness."

I don't say anything.

"You OK?" Adam asks, his eyes searching mine.

I take my books away from my front and show him my mess.

"Poor you. Your mom was just in here—I guess she dropped off new clothes?"

"Yeah."

"What is it?"

"Sloppy joe," I tell him. "It was pretty awful. They all laughed." I don't say who, but he knows.

"I skipped lunch today," he says, bringing his fingers up to his lips, smoking a joint. "Sorry I wasn't there to help." He's sincere, not smirking at all.

Adam is one confusing guy. He can be so nice. Like when Grandpa died. I had forgotten about that until this moment. He came with his father one night during *shivah*. Spent the whole time by my side. Alexis was there, too, but that night she mostly stayed in the kitchen helping with food and cleaning up. Adam stuck to me like glue. He didn't say much, but if I got at all teary, he kind of leaned into me or touched me lightly on the arm. At one point an old friend of Grandma's came over and pinched my cheek and said, "Your grandfather is in a better place now, dear." When she walked away, Adam said exactly what I was thinking—"Bullshit!"—and gave me a little hug.

"Good luck with your meeting," I say to him now, and go to change.

At the end of the day, my phone rings. I look, hoping for Alexis, but it's Marissa.

"Hello?" I say.

"I'm really sorry I laughed. So is Kendra. Can we take you out for a coffee or something? To make it up?"

"Oh, you don't have to. I'm fine," I say.

"Please?"

"Where are you?"

"We're standing right behind you!" she giggles, and I turn around, and there they are.

"I guess it *was* pretty funny," I say.

"We weren't laughing *at* you," Kendra says, "we were laughing *with* you!"

I roll my eyes. "As if!" But I laugh. Finally. "And thanks for getting the napkins and stuff," I tell them.

They sort of hug me, one on either side, and then we hook arms and march down the street to the little café/ice cream parlor near school. Marissa convinces me to get an iced coffee with vanilla ice cream in it. "It's how they do it in Israel," she says. We all get them.

"I'm moving to Israel!" I declare after my first few sips, being very careful not to spill a single drop on my clean black shirt.

"Me too!" says Marissa. "Right of return—they have to take us; we're Jewish!"

"Damn," says Kendra. "I'm converting!"

"But wouldn't you miss your dad's peanut butter and bacon sandwiches?" asks Marissa.

"Well, I don't have to go the whole hog," says Kendra. "Get it?"

"We get it, we get it," says Marissa, and we all laugh.

It goes on like that for more than an hour—silly jokes, happy banter—but the whole time I am acutely aware that they are not Alexis and that Alexis is not there.

CHAPTER 11

STREAMERS

After school Thursday, I head up to McKelvy's room to retake the Katrina quiz. This time I really read those chapters and then looked up more stuff. It's horrific. We have to do a long report soon, and I'm definitely going to do mine on New Orleans and Katrina.

"I changed the questions, so if you got them from other kids, forget about it," McKelvy says.

"I did not cheat. You know I wouldn't do that!" I am truly insulted.

"I know," he says, with a tinge of doubt.

I show *him*. I'm done in five minutes, he grades it right away, and I get them all right.

"Good for you, Rachel."

"Horrible topic," I say to him. "I can't believe all the poverty there still and how much those people need."

"Sure is awful, Rachel. I'm glad you see that. Speaking of need, you ready to go to Union tomorrow?"

Oops. Totally forgot.

First reaction: What a pain. Don't want to do it.

Second reaction: I know in my heart I should. *Tikkun olam*, repairing the world.

Third: What else do I have to do on Friday afternoon? Nothing.

"Sure," I say.

McKelvy gives me the rundown on the school. The kids are mostly poor; something like 75 percent are on free lunch. The teachers are good and dedicated, but they need as much help as they can get. Since I leave at one-twenty on Fridays, I can give them a full hour.

"Want me to go with you?" McKelvy asks. "I have a free period; I could take you down."

I would love it if he came. But I should be able to do this by myself. "I'll be fine," I say.

"You can catch the bus right outside, the number four."

I know that bus. Alexis and I used to take it all the time to go shopping at Morrison's.

On the bus the next afternoon, I find myself thinking about Alexis and feeling so blue. Stop it! I'm on my way to help some kids who really need it. Focus on that. *Tikkun olam*, which I heard about from the rabbi, of course. First when I was little, and later, a few months after Grandpa died.

I was alone at temple one Friday after school, setting up for a coffeehouse in the small social hall. Alexis and I were trying out Youth Group and had volunteered to do the decorations, but she was home sick that day.

So there I was trying to hang up the streamers by myself—it is really hard to hang streamers alone! I'd tape one end of the streamer to the ceiling, standing on a ladder that the janitor had given me with all kinds of warnings ("Do not stand on the top step, young lady"), and then I'd move the ladder, go back and get the end of the streamer, and carefully, without ripping it, twist it and take it where I'd put the ladder, climb up the ladder, and tape the streamer to the ceiling there. It was taking forever. I was up on the ladder when my phone beeped. I rushed down to get it out of my bag, hoping it was Alexis saying she was feeling better or hadn't really been sick at all and that she was coming over to help. I slipped off the ladder, crashing it—and me—to the floor. Landed right on my knee. Man did that hurt.

I slid to get my phone, even with my knee throbbing. But it wasn't Alexis. This girl Leslie, who was a senior and had said she might come help, had texted:

Can't come. Sorry. Violin lesson ran over. Gotta go home.

A sharp pain shot through my knee.

"Shit!" I yelled. "Shit, shit, fu—"

At that exact moment the rabbi walked into the social hall.

I was beyond mortified to have cursed in front of him. He ignored it, though. "Pretty tough doing this on your own, huh, Rachel?"

I nodded and started crying. I couldn't help it. I was frustrated, my knee was killing me, and I cried easily back then.

"You hurt yourself?"

"My knee," I sobbed.

He went to the kitchen and got me an ice pack, told me

to hold it on for ten minutes and then he'd help me put up the streamers.

"You don't have to do that," I said. "A rabbi shouldn't have to put up streamers!"

"*Nu?* You think a rabbi can't put up streamers?" he said in a fake Yiddish accent. "I've been putting up streamers since before they were even invented, *Rachelleh*. I was putting up streamers for Moses. You know, when he came down with the Ten Commandments? Streamers."

It was a stupid joke—it didn't even make sense—but it was the way he said it, with that Yiddish accent and a half smile. Cheered me up right away. He could do that. I tell myself now that I was not naive. Everyone felt—still feels—that way about him.

Could I be wrong about him now? Or *was* I naive then?

As I sat there icing my knee, the rabbi in a chair next to me, we talked about this and that.

"How is your grandmother doing?" he asked me after a while. I knew he visited her every week. So he was totally aware of how badly she was doing. He was actually asking me how *I* was doing.

"It's horrible, Rabbi," I said. "She's nothing like she used to be. It's like we're all in a really bad dream and we can't wake up." Grandma had turned from a happy, energetic eighty-year-old who went to the gym and did yoga into a decrepit old lady, just like that. My parents' fighting began then, too. It's like Grandpa's death started an avalanche of sorrow.

He nodded, didn't say anything.

"Why would God do this, Rabbi? To Grandpa? To Grandma?

To us?" I immediately felt bad about saying that—it was blasphemous. The rabbi shook his head, stroked his beard, frowned.

"I'm sorry, Rabbi, I shouldn't have said that."

"No, you shouldn't be sorry," he said. "I don't blame you for asking. It's exactly what I would ask. The thing is, I think you're going to be surprised by my answer. And I'm not sure you're going to like it."

"Hang on! I'll help you!" the bus driver yells out, breaking into my memories. He puts the bus in park, closes the front door, and walks to the back. I turn around. There's a guy in a wheelchair coming up the ramp. The driver has to strap the wheelchair in place in the back. I watch how carefully he does it, joking quietly with the man, who doesn't look embarrassed, but I can't imagine why not.

I should not be staring. I turn around.

"Say whatever you want, Rabbi," I had told him. "I can take it."

The rabbi furrowed his brow, stroked his beard again. "So some rabbis might say in a situation like this that God doesn't give us anything we can't handle. Others might say that God has a plan that we can't know—we see only the back of the tapestry, the different threads woven together; it's only at the end of our lives that the beautiful picture on the other side is revealed."

Wait a minute, I thought. If that's so, that God is weaving the tapestry and only God can see the picture, then do we have no part in creating the design?

"Rachel, I don't think God had anything to do with your grandfather's death."

"Really? Then who did?"

He got up, walked around for a minute, taped up the end of the streamer I had been working on when I fell off the ladder, and then came back and sat down. He put his hand on my head, lightly.

"Rachel, your grandfather died because he had an undiagnosed heart problem. His heart burst in his chest. It was not an act of God. It was faulty plumbing." As hard as it was for me to hear this horrible detail that no one else had told me (my grandfather's heart burst in his chest?), it was also sort of reassuring. God hadn't killed him. But thinking back on this, I wonder if he wasn't wrong to say that to me. Was it his to tell?

"And Grandma?" I'd asked.

"Your poor grandmother. She loved your grandfather so much. They had a real love story. Did you know that?"

"Sort of." I knew that they met right after the Holocaust, when Grandpa came to this country. Grandpa was eighteen or so. Grandma was really young, not quite sixteen. My age.

"They did. They were each other's first and only loves. He died so suddenly, so unexpectedly, I'm surprised it didn't kill—no, I won't say that. But, Rachel, as tragic as it is for your grandmother, I envy them their love story."

Why would he envy them their love story? Wasn't he happy with his wife? I wondered.

"Still, believe me, I don't envy her the torturous grief she has now. Poor, poor lady. If I believed in a God that would do that to her, Rachel, I wouldn't, couldn't, be a rabbi."

I stared at him.

"I couldn't even be a believing Jew."

"So, what . . . How do I . . . I'm not even sure I know what to ask."

"Where does God fit in to all of this, and where do you fit in to all of this?"

"I guess so."

"I think there are many answers to that question, and also only one. Remember the story of Rabbi Hillel and the pagan? When the pagan challenges Rabbi Hillel to tell him everything about Judaism while standing on one foot, Hillel says, " 'What is hateful to you, do not do to others; all the rest is commentary.' "

I nodded. He was in full-fledged preaching-rabbi mode now.

"Hillel then said, 'Now go and study.' And I would say to you, 'Now go to work.' "

"Huh?"

"Your grandmother needs your love and your attention. She needs you to spend time with her. Keep her company. Love her. Isn't that what you would want someone to do for you if you were grief-stricken?"

"Yes." Yes.

"And you know about *tikkun olam*, right?"

I nodded. "Repairing the world."

"The world is broken," he said. "It's not a perfect place. So it is everyone's duty to help fix it, Rachel. *I* believe the best way to do so is one person at a time, even one act at a time."

I took the ice pack off my knee.

"So is that what God wants me to do?" I asked the rabbi. "To help repair the world by loving my grandmother?"

"Is that what you think? That's what's important—what you think."

I knew it was. I resolved to spend more time with Grandma, to love her up so she would come back to herself.

The rabbi helped me hang up all the streamers and arrange the tables. By the time we left, the room looked perfect.

Now, a year later, my grandmother is a colossal mess, even though I spent tons of time with her.

Alexis is a creature from another planet.

My parents are on the brink of divorce.

And the rabbi fucked someone on the *bima*.

The bus driver calls out my stop. I am right in front of Union Elementary School. I look at the building, take a step toward it. And then I turn around and walk in the opposite direction.

CHAPTER 12

UNION

I walk down the street away from the school, away from Morrison's and the Red Eagle Diner. I am walking fast, not thinking about where I'm going. Soon I find myself on a block lined with row houses and small apartment buildings. I have never been in this neighborhood before. There are a whole lot more people outside in the middle of the day than there would be on my block. There's a lady sweeping her porch; she's got Spanish pop music playing. There are two guys working on a car engine. And another guy sitting on a step drinking a can of beer. "*Chica!*" he says to me as I pass. I nod, walk quickly by. I feel too *something* to be here. What is it? Too rich? Too white? Too Jewish? I tuck my Star of David necklace inside my shirt, zip up my jacket.

I cross the street and walk back the way I came, even faster. It's not that I don't feel safe; it's that I feel noticeable. I put my head down as I pass "*Chica!*" man, who has crossed to this side of the street with his beer can. But he is talking to a woman in a black leather jacket and stiletto boots and, thankfully, ignores me.

I end up back at Union, staring at it. I know I should go in.

Right now, so I'm not too late. But the building puts me off: the bricks are dirty, most are cracked, some are missing. Above the main door is graffiti that they'd tried to scrub off, but they didn't completely succeed. I can only make out a few letters, but my mind fills in the rest: SCHOOL SUCKS.

The place scares me. But how can I not go to the reading lab? I have to honor my commitment. I am not a self-centered hypocrite like some people I know. Also, if I don't go in, what would I say to McKelvy? What excuse could I make?

It is not a noble reason, for sure, that has me walking very slowly toward the front door.

Two women are leaning against the building, talking. I watch them from the sidewalk; they don't see me. One of them is nodding, the other shaking her head. An argument? An impromptu parent-teacher conference? But I obviously have the situation totally wrong, because all of a sudden they break into laughter. I stare at them, confused. They stop laughing and stare back at me.

"Can I help you?" one of them shouts.

I pick up my pace, relieved that my hand has been forced. I have to do the right thing. Even if it's for the wrong reasons.

"I'm here to volunteer in the reading lab."

I'm sure they're going to give me the business, but then they smile. One says, "OK, dear, go inside and tell them at the office. They'll get you to the right place."

"Thank you," I say.

I press the buzzer, and someone says, "Yes?"

"I'm here to volunteer in the reading lab."

The door buzzes, then clicks, and I open it up. I walk into the lobby, which is cheerfully decorated with splatter paintings on the walls. I head toward the office, straight down the hall. Two little girls come skipping toward me holding hands, singing.

"Hi, Mrs. Oberdorfer!" they shout to a teacher.

"Hi, munchkins!" she says. "Please walk."

The three office ladies are sitting at their desks working and do not look up. I clear my throat.

"You the girl from the high school?" asks one of them, getting up.

I nod.

"Sign in here, then you should hurry downstairs. The period has started already. Go down the stairs, turn right, and go to the end of the hall. You'll see Mrs. Glick's haven."

"She calls it her 'haven in Hades' because it's in the basement," one of the others says.

As I walk down the stairs and through the hall, I see why they call it Hades. It is dark and dismal down here.

But when I get to the reading lab, it is full of light. There are lamps all over the room: a floor lamp shaped like a rocket ship, another like a big crayon, a third, bright pink one; there are Winnie the Pooh, Cat in the Hat, and Mickey Mouse desk lamps on brightly colored tables. There's a pirate wall light, and a pink Cinderella clock with pink bulbs circling it.

All over the walls are posters about reading. Basketball stars reading with kids, kids reading to dogs, an alligator with glasses reading to other alligators.

There are tables and chairs but also beanbag chairs on the floor: one shaped like a lion, one like a car, the rest big colorful blobs.

No one notices me. All over the room are pairs of kids and

adults reading, some at the tables, the rest on the floor. Most are women, though there is one older man. The adults are Hispanic, black, white. One of the women has two kids with her, a boy and a girl, and for some reason I know it's Mrs. Glick, the reading teacher, not one of the volunteers. She's got pink reading glasses on, and she's wearing black pants and a bright blue scoop-neck sweater. She has short jet-black hair with silver streaks in it. I go over to her.

"Excuse me, I'm Rachel."

The lady picks up her head. "Oh, good, Rachel. I was worried you weren't coming." She gives me an appraising look, doesn't say anything more.

"I'm sorry. The bus was slow."

She nods, but I can tell she doesn't believe me. "Sorry, but I don't have time to give you all the instructions—I don't want to take time away from Ashley." She nods at the little girl with her. "Why don't you take Randy here and read to him. If you can stay after school, I'll give you the lowdown."

"OK," I say.

"I'm Mrs. Glick, by the way. The reading teacher."

"I know. I mean, hi." I promise myself never to get here late again.

She turns to the boy with her. "Randy, this is Rachel—I'm sorry, Rachel what?"

"Greenberg," I say. "I'm Rachel Greenberg." I look at Randy.

"Randy, tell Rachel your whole name."

Randy looks up at me. He is about eight, I'd say, with red hair and freckles, a round face. "I'm Randy Gamez," he says in a loud voice.

"Randy, why don't you take Rachel over to the shelf you like and pick out a book for her to read to you? Then you can go sit wherever you want."

Randy grabs my hand. His feels sweaty, sticky. I look down; it's really dirty. I want to pull away, but I don't. The shelf he takes me to is lined with books about cars. He picks one out, seemingly at random, and then takes me over to the beanbag chair shaped like a car.

"You like cars?" I ask him.

"I LOVE cars," he practically shouts, and grins at me. He hands me the book, and I start to read it to him.

"This is the hood of the car. Open it up. What is inside? The engine!" I look at him, sure he must be bored, but he is riveted. I keep going, reading about pistons and rods and steering wheels, and I kind of zone out as I'm reading. Finally I reach the end:

"And that is how cars go!"

I look at Randy. He looks back at me and smiles. It is a satisfied smile. OK.

I tell him to put this book back and get another one. This time he's very serious about choosing a new book—he picks one up, looks at it, and puts it carefully back.

Finally, he finds the right one and starts back toward me. For the first time I see his T-shirt. It's green, has a picture of a cactus and a snake on it, and says, WILD WEST ADVENTURE. ELIJAH'S BAR MITZVAH. APRIL 10, 2010. Is Randy Jewish? How can such a poor kid be Jewish?

"I haven't read this one before!" Randy yells, all excited.

"You noticed!" Mrs. Glick says, looking up from the book she's reading to Ashley. "I had to get you some new car books, Randy! But let's use our inside voice, OK?"

Randy nods and sits back down next to me, this time cuddling closer.

I read him a total of five books about cars. I have learned some things about cars I never knew I wanted to learn. I'm relieved when Mrs. Glick says, "Time's up, everyone. Kids, put your books back. And have a great weekend."

The other volunteers say good-bye to their kids, most of them with hugs, and leave. But I stay so Mrs. Glick (is *she* Jewish?) can give me the lowdown.

"So, what did you think?"

"Well, I read him all of those books about cars. He seemed to love hearing them, and I think he got what I was reading. I should have asked him some questions."

"Next time, that's what you'll do. He wants to learn to read, but it hasn't happened yet. His classroom teacher has worked with him, and she wasn't making any progress, so she asked if we could help, too."

"What grade is he in?"

"Second."

"Huh." I was reading *Harry Potter* in second grade.

"Yeah, and he really should be in third grade—he's almost nine. But he didn't quite get to school until he was, I don't know, six and a half."

"Why not?"

"Oh, it's a long story. He's got—his home life is not so great."

"That's an understatement," says another voice.

I hadn't realized another adult was still in the room. She's at a computer.

"Rachel, this is Mrs. Washington. She's the other reading teacher."

"Hi," I say.

"Thanks for working with Randy," says Mrs. Washington.

"So can you tell me a little about him, or is it secret?"

"It's not a secret, exactly," Mrs. Glick says, "but I don't think you need to know that much."

"OK," I say. And then, because I do want to know, I try to sell myself. "My mom is a social worker. She works with foster kids and their families. I kind of know some stuff."

The two teachers exchange a look, but before they can answer me, I blurt out, "Is Randy Jewish?"

"Randy? No, not that I know of," Mrs. Glick says. "Why?"

I feel my face get red. "He was wearing a T-shirt from a bar mitzvah."

"Goodwill," says Mrs. Washington.

"Actually, that was one of mine, from a family bar mitzvah. I keep a supply here. I gave it to Randy one day when he needed a change of clothes. So let me tell you how we work here."

Mrs. Glick takes me through the program. The kids who come to the reading lab have all been tested. They don't have learning disabilities, but they either aren't reading or are reading below grade level.

"Kids without learning disabilities but with problems reading often get lost in the cracks. That's why I started this program. Sometimes all it takes is a way to help them crack the code, speaking of cracks."

"*Speaking* of . . . ," says Mrs. Washington.

Mrs. Glick frowns.

What? Crack?

"Anyways," says Mrs. Glick, "with certain kids it's pairing

visual images with words; with others it's helping them hear the sounds of the words. And with some it's a mystery until it happens."

"Randy's got no one at home who reads to him," says Mrs. Washington.

"Probably," says Mrs. Glick, shooting Mrs. Washington a look. "So it might just be a matter of as much exposure to words as the school can give him. He knows his letters but can't put them together as words. And then one day, we hope, it will click."

She shows me around the room, where the different levels of books are, how they are grouped by subject. There are report forms I'll have to fill out each week.

"It's a real challenge," Mrs. Glick says to me as we are saying good-bye. "But when it works, well, that feeling is so amazing—you could tie it up and give it to me as a present any day."

I nod. I don't know what to say. I wish I could stay in her haven forever, doing good, repairing the world, not thinking about my own stuff.

"Thanks," I say to her.

"No, thank *you*," she says.

"Good-bye!" says Mrs. Washington. "Have a good weekend."

"I'm going to try," I tell them.

CHAPTER 13

BAREFOOT AND IN THE KITCHEN

I have not heard from Jake since he left. He warned me, but still. Saturday I wait around for him to call or text. He's coming home today. I'm not sure what time.

So I wait. And I wait some more.

And I could wait some more but
a girl can make the move and
this is not the old days and
this girl is pretty desperate for some
contact with a nice human being around her own age,
preferably male, preferably Jake.

"I'm going for a bike ride," I yell to my parents.

They both yell back, "Fine, be careful" at exactly the same time. For some reason that gives me hope.

I pedal fast. It's drizzling, but I don't care. I look for hills, going out of my way so I can pump hard going up and glide fast going down, careful to avoid the slick fallen leaves. It feels good to work out. I'm so focused on *moving* that I don't realize the rain has picked up until it starts pouring buckets. By the time I get to Jake's house, Sir Walter is making not-happy-at-all squeaks and I am a drowned rat. I take off my helmet.

Helmet hair to end all helmet hair. I ring the bell anyway.

Mrs. Schmidt opens the door. Not Jake. "Rachel, what are you doing riding your bike in the rain like this? Are you OK?"

I nod vigorously. "I'm fine. Is Jake here?"

"He's still away—at the swim competition." She looks at her watch. "I have to get him at the bus station in—oh, in about an hour. He's going to call when he gets in."

"How did he do? At the meet, I mean?"

She is standing with the door partway open. I am getting wetter by the second, if that's even possible. I can see why she's not asking me in. The wind is blowing the rain in on her. I move back to leave.

"He did very well—mostly first places, a few second. He had fun."

I don't say anything. What if he's met another girl? There is a long, awkward pause.

"Do you want to come in and dry off? You can come with me to pick up Jake." I am embarrassed for Jake to see me like this, and I should say no, but I *am* shivering, and being dry seems like a very good idea.

"Come around the back, if you don't mind," she says.

"Of course!" I say.

"I'll open the garage door, and you can put your bike in there."

I have never been in Jake's house before. She leads me to the laundry room. "I'll bring you a robe. Why don't you put your clothes in the dryer?"

"Thank you!" She is so sweet. I stand in the laundry room shivering, until she hands me a white terry-cloth robe, the kind they have in fancy hotels.

"Would you like a cup of tea?"

"Yes, please."

"Irish Breakfast or Lemon Ginger?"

I sure don't need caffeine. I'm too jazzed up as it is. "Lemon Ginger. Thank you."

"Honey?"

"Yes?"

"Um, do you want honey for your tea?"

Erg. "Yes, please," I say.

I strip off my soaking wet clothes, all of them, even my bra, and throw them in the dryer. I don't want to shrink my bra, so I put the dryer on delicate.

The robe is soft and cuddly; I wrap it tightly around me and go join Jake's mom.

While she makes the tea she chatters, tells me they have barely heard from Jake since he's been gone, that he was so obsessed with the swimming, he hadn't called them at all. Just a few texts. That's how he gets, she says, and it makes me feel a little better.

I am warm and cozy in this kitchen. It's got a cherrywood island in the middle, a floor that matches, covered with a few braided rugs here and there, walls painted a light buttercream, with family pictures hung everywhere. I bet Jake's parents aren't fighting; I am sure Dr. Schmidt isn't sleeping on the couch. I doubt Jake spends his days and nights worried that his parents are going to get divorced.

The only thing is, there is something weird about the photos. In lots of the pictures there are four people: Jake, his parents, and a younger boy who looks a lot like Jake, but not. Something about the way he looks, kind of vague and never really looking at the camera, makes me think twice and not ask Jake's mom who he is. Jake has never mentioned a younger brother, and I have never seen one with them.

Mrs. Schmidt asks me a million questions: about school, what subjects I like best (English and history); about where I think I might want to go to college (no idea, but I throw out some names that I have ready for when adults ask—the three Bs, I call them: Barnard, Brown, and Bard; they're all totally different, that much I know, but she gives them each respectable nods). Then, of course, she asks what I want to do when I grow up (also no idea, but I throw out some possibilities: journalist, social worker, college professor). Finally I manage to ask, "What does Jake want to be? Do you know?"

She shrugs. "He used to want to be a doctor, like his father, but lately he's been very much into economics; he talks about figuring out a way to abolish third-world debt, that kind of thing. I—I know I'm his mother, but I really think Jake could do anything he put his mind to."

I nod. "He's smart," I say, brilliantly.

"He sure is, and very adult, really." She shakes her head a little and glances up at the wall. I look where she's looking. It's a picture of Jake and the other boy.

Before I can ask anything, she turns to me and says, "Barely cracks a book and still gets all As."

I thought Jake was one of those people who studied all the time. "Really? What does he do when the rest of us are doing homework?"

"I'm not sure. Reads blogs, I think. Plays chess online. Swims, works out."

OK, he's perfect. I know he is.

"He's not perfect. You should see his room! It's a disaster area!"

Had I said that aloud, or was she reading my mind? We sit there for a few minutes, kind of awkwardly, and she finally says, "He can be moody, too. I worry about him sometimes, that he doesn't talk more. I mean, he has some major things he should talk about. . . ."

It is my opening, but the phone rings.

"Jake? You're here already? Good. Let me—give me a few minutes; I have to make sure Rachel's clothes are dry and . . ."

Oh, I can just imagine what he is saying on the other end of the phone. Rachel? Rachel is there? I smile.

"Yes, Rachel rode her bike over here to see you, and she was soaking wet, so . . . We're sitting in the kitchen drinking tea."

Mrs. Schmidt frowns, shakes her head. I hear Jake's raised voice, but I can't hear what he's saying.

"Yes, I told you, in the kitchen. Jake, I'm sorry, I—" Mrs. Schmidt shoots me a look that I can't read. She hangs up without saying anything. Walks out of the kitchen into the laundry room.

"Dry enough, I'd say," she shouts to me. I walk in, take my still very damp clothes from her, and get dressed while she waits in the kitchen. It is disgusting putting these wet clothes back on. I don't bother with my bra, stuff it in my pocket.

When I walk back into the kitchen, Jake's mom looks at me, embarrassed, and says uncomfortably, "Jake, uh, said there were a few things he needs to do, uh, on the way home, so if it's OK, I'll drop you off first and then pick him up. OK?"

What? What could he have to do that I couldn't go along with them? Why doesn't he want to see me?

I look out the window. It's slowed down a bit. "It's not raining that much anymore, so seeing as how these clothes are still wet and I'll get your car all wet, I'll ride my bike home."

"No, let me drive you," she says halfheartedly.

"No, it's fine, really." I leave quickly before she can protest anymore.

"Rachel?" she calls after me.

I just wave, smile, grab my bike, and jump on the seat. Everything squishes as I pedal away.

The sky is dark. I pray it doesn't start to thunder and lightning. I don't want to be struck by lightning. Or a falling branch. Or a car. I pedal fast.

It starts to rain harder.

I pedal harder. My heart is pounding, not from exertion but from fear.

I can barely see more than a foot in front of me.

At least the cars have their lights on, so I can see *them*. They sure as hell can't see me.

I take the shortest route, avoid hills, ride as fast as I can without skidding, slipping, falling.

Finally I get home.

Without getting killed.

That's good.

Right?

CHAPTER 14

TRUMPED

My phone is ringing and someone is knocking on my bedroom door at the same time. It's only eleven o'clock on Sunday morning, and I don't have Sunday school. I want to sleep!

But wait—what if it's Jake? I texted him last night—`How was the meet?`—and last I looked (at two a.m.) he hadn't answered. I just don't get it.

By the time I find my phone under the bed, it's stopped.

"Rachel," Mom is saying.

"What?" I yell, fumbling with my phone to see who it was.

"Grandma's here! Come down and eat brunch with us."

Was this a plan? No one told me.

I look at my phone. Alexis. Lex called me? Wow. I wonder why. I will not get my hopes up. She probably needs a homework assignment or something. But nothing from Jake.

"You coming?" It's Mom again.

"I have to get dressed and stuff. I'll be down soon. Start without me."

"Can I come in for a second?"

"OK."

Mom opens the door, sticks her head in.

"She's good this morning," she whispers. Why is she whispering? Grandma is downstairs and half deaf. "Like her old self. Thought you'd want to see her like this, you know?" Mom is smiling.

Don't be too happy, Mom. It's not going to last. This is what I want to say. But I just nod and tell her, "Great. Thanks, I'll be down in a minute."

I call Alexis back while I'm peeing. Like the old days.

"What's up?" she says.

"You called me," I say with a little bit of irritation.

"Yeah, I thought, maybe you want to go shopping? I need new jeans and stuff. Thought we could go downtown. To Morrison's, or maybe to that store that has used jeans? Or to the mall?"

"Eddie's Exchange," I say.

"What?"

"The store downtown that has used jeans."

"Yeah, I know. Hold on. I've got another call."

I want to go shopping with Alexis, but I don't actually want to miss the good Grandma moment. Can I do both? I am going to do both.

"So?" Alexis is back.

"Yeah, I could go in, like, an hour or two?"

"OK."

"My grandmother's here. And Mom says she's *good*, Alexis."

Silence.

"So we're having brunch. Listen, Lex, I really want to say again that I'm sorry about your parents. I wish I could have helped—and could help now. I really do."

She doesn't say anything. Did the line go dead?

"You there?" I ask.

"Yeah."

"OK. Um." What? Did she not hear me? "So should I call you when Grandma leaves?"

"Yeah." Her phone beeps. "No, no," she says. "I've got to take this. I'll call *you*."

"Great," I squeal. Oh God. I am pathetic. I stand up and almost drop the phone in the toilet.

I wash my face, try to scrub away my sleep and my insecurities. (Boy, that would be a great invention: a soap that gets rid of acne AND self-doubt! I'd make a million bucks.) My hair is a curly mess. If I brush it, it will only get frizzy. So I pull it back into a ponytail, which will make Grandma happy—the better to see my face, she'll say, if she really *is* with it. I put on jeans and a shirt that Grandma bought for me. It's a deep wine red, and it looks good on me.

"Rachelleh, don't you look beautiful!" Grandma says as I walk into the dining room, where Mom has set the table as if it's a special occasion.

"Thanks, Grandma."

"I gave you that shirt! Looks good on you!" she says. "And with your hair pulled back, I can see your beautiful face!"

I lean down and give Grandma a big kiss on the cheek, and she kisses me back. I breathe in the smell of her. Charlie perfume and lox. I give her another kiss and rub my cheek against hers. Her skin is so, so soft.

"Grandma," I whisper into her ear, "I love you." Tears fill my eyes.

"I love you, too, Rachel," she whispers into my ear, and I feel like all is right with the world for this moment. I hold on to it, my cheek against hers. I squeeze her tight, but not too tight. Don't want to break anything. I never, ever want to let her go.

But I have to. Because she starts reaching for her whitefish salad. Grandma wants to eat!

I sit down at the table and grab myself a whole-wheat-with-everything bagel and spread it with cream cheese. Mom is beaming at Grandma while simultaneously giving me a raised eyebrow. My mother the multitasker. Too much cream cheese is what that eyebrow is saying. Tough. I take two pieces of lox and a red onion. I will have to brush my teeth three times before going shopping with Alexis, but I don't care.

Dad is slicing the extra bagels to put in the freezer and starts telling a story about his day in New York last week.

"So I'm walking down the street, around Madison and Sixty-third—"

"What were you doing *there*?" Mom asks, a little suspiciously.

"It was after my meeting," he says cheerfully, "which was on Lex and about Seventieth, and I thought I'd walk to the bus station, and I hear this guy say angrily on his cell phone, 'My driver was supposed to be here, but the Secret Service wouldn't let him through, so now I'm going to be really late.' So I turn around to look at this guy, but there, walking out of a store on Madison, is—want to guess?"

"Secret Service?" Mom says. "So someone in government, right?"

"Right," says Dad.

"Do we like this person?" asks Grandma.

"Yes," says Dad. "We love her."

"The first lady?" Grandma says.

"Bingo!" says Dad.

"Wow," says Mom. "Very cool." And she gives Dad a huge grin.

"I wanted to say something, but her people whisked her into a car immediately."

"What would you have said?" Grandma asks.

"Hi?" Dad answers, and laughs, and Mom punches him lightly on the arm.

Oh. I am happier than I've been in a long time.

After we're done with the bagels and lox, Mom brings out some vanilla yogurt and her granola. I am full, but I can't help myself. I won't try on any jeans later!

"Want to play cards?" Grandma asks, and Mom and Dad say "sure" immediately.

"I can't. I'm going shopping with Alexis," I say. "She's going to call."

"So play until she calls," Mom says.

"OK."

We play partners Pitch, me and Mom against Dad and Grandma. It's our usual teams because Dad and I are the best players, and so the teams are evenly matched, but today Mom and I keep winning. I look at Dad's face, and I can tell it's bad luck with the cards. It's not that Grandma is messing up.

Finally, when Mom and I win for the fourth time, I suggest we switch partners so I'm with Grandma. This is a hairy thing, because Dad and Mom usually fight if they're partners. But today that's not the problem. I deal and am ready to make a two-bid in spades. I have the ace, the jack, and a seven. But Mom bids two, and then, when it gets to Grandma, she bids three. She must have a great suit, probably diamonds. I don't have any. Dad passes, I pass. When Grandma says "spades," I know we're in trouble. No way should she have bid three spades if I have the ace and the jack. What could she have that made her bid three?

I get nothing on the draw. We're screwed.

She plays the nine, a lead that says, I've got nothing. I throw the ace, and we get trash. I lead non-trump, Grandma throws the two of spades on it, and Dad takes it with his queen. I look at her face; she doesn't register that she did something stupid.

Dad leads the king of spades; I have nothing to do but give him my jack. We're going down. And then Grandma gives him the ten, even though later she throws the four.

I see Mom and Dad exchange glances, and Mom starts to tear up. Grandma is disappearing again.

To lighten things up and maybe get Grandma back, I start singing, "We're going down, down, down," but she doesn't register anything.

We do go down three; Dad and Mom get three. Mom notes the score and deals the next hand.

"What happened?" Grandma asks.

"We went down, Grandma. No big deal."

"Was it my fault?"

I shake my head, but I can't bring myself to lie out loud.

Grandma looks at me in confusion. (I wish Alexis would call. Please call, Alexis. Now.) Grandma's eyes start to puddle.

"No, don't worry, Grandma. We'll come back."

"No we won't," she says, and starts crying. "I can't do this without Leonard. Where's Leonard?"

Leonard being Grandpa. I reach over and take Grandma's hand, and stroke it. It feels as soft as always, but more fragile. I can see her veins.

Mom gets up, fills a glass with water, and brings it to Grandma. Dad gives the cards a couple of shuffles and then puts them back in the box.

"I want to go home," Grandma whimpers. "See Leonard. Where's Leonard?"

Mom coos to her, "You'll feel better soon, Mom. Drink this, that's a girl." Mom gently pats her on the back.

Dad walks over to the CD player. I see what he picks: Grandma's favorite, *Ella & Louis*. Good choice, Dad. But the minute the first song comes on, Ella singing, "I thought I'd found the man of my dreams," Grandma starts sobbing.

"Nice going," Mom says to Dad. "What the hell were you thinking?" She turns off the CD player.

"Sorry! I tried," Dad grumbles. "I have to work anyway."

"Fine!" Mom says. "I'm taking Mother home. I'll stay with her until she's OK."

She looks at me. "Have a good time with Alexis."

Ignores my father.

Rushes out. I don't even get to give Grandma a kiss.

Dad starts doing the dishes, banging them loudly as he puts them in the dishwasher.

"I'll do it," I tell him.

"Thanks."

He goes down to the basement to his office. I put away the leftover food, stealing a little bit more whitefish salad, load the dishwasher, hand-wash the big platters. The warm water and suds are soothing. Sometimes a mindless chore is just the thing.

Better than waiting for Alexis to call. It's almost two o'clock, an hour and a half past the time when I said I could go. But who's counting? I wait another fifteen minutes, and then I finally call her. She doesn't answer.

I yell down and ask Dad if he'll give me a little driving lesson. "Yeah, maybe later, honey," he answers.

I wipe off the kitchen counter and decide it needs more. I move everything off it—the canisters, the coffeemaker, the blender, the toaster oven, the utensil holder, and put it all on the kitchen table. Then I get out a clean sponge and scrub the whole counter. Hard. Then go at the sink. The faucet. The windowsill behind the sink. I dry the counter, put everything back, rearranging it all how I think it should go.

Alexis still hasn't called.

I take out the copper cleaner and attack all the pots with copper bottoms. The great thing about copper cleaner is that it shines up the copper immediately. You don't even have to rub hard. This is such a great metaphor for what I wish I could do in my life!

Why *isn't* she calling? Or texting? Why isn't Jake? Maybe he emailed!

I check. Nothing there or on Facebook.

I think about scrubbing my bathtub, but that would be way over the top, so I do something that is also way over the top, desperate, and I call Alexis again. Surprise, surprise, she picks up her phone.

"Yeah?"

"Hey," I say.

"Who is it?"

She can see who it is. "It's me, Rachel."

"Oh. I'm on the other line. What is it?"

"Aren't we going shopping?"

"Can't."

"Call me back," I say. But I can't tell if she's clicked back to her other call already.

I go scrub my bathtub.

Dad and I back down the driveway a few times, which is hard, because our driveway is long and has a curve in it. Then he shows me how to parallel-park. I'm going to need more lessons. Afterward I take a nap. When I hear Mom come back from Grandma's, I go downstairs.

"How is she?"

She shakes her head. Her eyes are all red.

"You OK?" I ask her.

She shakes her head again. "I let myself get my hopes up. It's just, I thought, maybe she's back, you know? Maybe it was just grief this whole time. But when I got her home, she was so confused she almost peed on the footstool instead of in the toilet. I had to call an agency and have an aide stay with her. Oh, Rachel, I shouldn't have told you that, about the peeing."

"It's OK," I say, but I wonder if I'll ever get that image out of my head.

"Where's your father?"

"Working."

"Right." Mom goes into her bedroom. I hear her crying. Should I go in? I figure if she wanted to cry in front of me, she would have stayed out here.

I go up to my room. Open my math book. Not for the first

time, I wonder how someone as smart as I am can be so clueless about math.

Question: If one girl has twenty-six math problems and it takes her ten minutes to do the first one, and she gets the wrong answer, how many minutes would it take her to do all twenty-six problems correctly?

Answer: Googolplex minutes.

Better answer: Infinity minutes.

Best answer: Zero minutes.

CHAPTER 15

ACTION, ACTION, WE WANT ACTION!

I have to push myself through the mob watching the cheerleaders doing their thing in front of the school.

"Action, action, we want action! A-C-T! I-O-N!"

I am guessing there is a really big football game on Friday for them to start the pepping on Monday. I don't follow football, and I've never been to a game. I am not starting now. But I like the motto.

Really like it.

I will take it on as mine. My motto, my mantra, my reason for living. Forget *kavanah*, forget intention.

"Action, action, I want action. A-C-T. I-O-N," I shout along.

I walk into school and down through the halls, which are quiet and empty because everyone is standing outside cheering. Or almost everyone. The geeks and the Goths are inside, like me. I am neither geek nor Goth; I am a girl who needs to get back her friend and her almost-boyfriend.

I have classes with Jake this morning. I will make him talk to me. And then I will talk to Alexis at lunch. Ask her why she dissed me. Again. I can't believe I waited all night and neither one called me.

But it's OK. I've got this.

Or not. English class, Jake is surrounded by a whole throng of guys. To say this is unusual is an understatement. Jake is a loner. Everyone likes him, but he's not a guy-friend kind of a guy. I like that about him. He's self-sufficient. But today he's got these guys in his thrall, telling them a story. Mrs. Thomas isn't here yet.

I walk over to Jake (Action, Action, I want Action . . .), but he says something and manages to pull the gang closer.

It's like he's using the other kids as a security wall against me. I listen in. He's telling them about the swim meet: "And then, in the last five seconds, I push really hard and—"

"Class, to your seats!" Mrs. Thomas says.

The scene repeats itself in study hall. Security wall intact, Jake. Way to go.

Aside from the sloppy-joe fiasco, it probably looks to everyone else like Alexis and I are fine. We still eat lunch together every day with Marissa and Kendra and some other kids. She doesn't talk to me much, but she doesn't talk to the others, either. Texts with her boyfriend. At least, I think that's who she texts with. And she usually leaves early to go outside with Adam or some other guy. I'm not sure what they do out there. Don't really want to know.

Today she's at our table before I am. I squeeze between her and Marissa, taking a chair from another table. When the rest of the kids are all distracted, I silently repeat my mantra, then turn to her, upbeat. "Hey, what happened yesterday?"

"What do you mean?"

"You called me to go shopping and"—trying to say this without whining, painfully aware that I am definitely whining—"and then you said you were going to call back, but you didn't. I felt bad."

"Oh, Rachel. It's not always all about you." She runs her fingers through her even shorter, even blonder hair. When did she do *that*?

"So what was it about?" I try to keep my voice level.

"A friend was in a car accident. Friend of the Boyfriend's. Hurt bad. I knew the kid from last summer. We used to"—pause, pause—"hang out." Get high?

"Oh boy, I'm sorry. Not that it was my fault. I mean—I mean—" (Oh, get ahold of yourself, Rachel.) "I'm sorry he was hurt. Is he going to be OK? Did he have a head injury?"

"Nah. A lot of broken bones. Legs and stuff."

"Oh, good."

She looks at me. "It's not good. He might lose a leg."

"Oh no! That's horrible, Lex. Is Mitch—Mustache—uh, your boyfriend—really upset?"

Alexis shrugs, looks upset in a different way.

"What is it?" I ask kindly.

"He isn't really talking to me about it."

"Is everything OK with you guys?"

She shrugs again.

"Is that a no?" I ask.

She nods slightly.

I'm sorry that she's upset, but I'm also happy she's confiding in me.

"Alexis, do you wanna talk about this? We could walk home—"

"Adam!" she yells, and jumps up and runs over to him. They talk for a few minutes, heads together, his arm lightly around her shoulder, and then together they leave the cafeteria.

Yeah, that went well.

Gym class is next. "There is a yearbook emergency," I tell the teacher. She looks at me, trying to figure out who the hell I am.

"I'm Rachel Greenberg. I'm on the yearbook staff, and . . ."

She nods, says, "Go, go, it's fine."

It's Jake's lunch period. I go to his locker. He's closing it when I tap him on the shoulder.

He spins around, sees me, and looks like a criminal caught in the act.

"You're going to have to talk to me eventually," I say in my best assertive yet flirty voice.

"Rachel," he says. "Hello." He's looking at me so impersonally, he might as well be saying, Will that be for here or to go?

"OK, what did I do wrong? Why are you ignoring me? Did you decide you don't like the way I kiss?"

"Shhh . . . ," he says.

"Why are you shutting me out?" I don't mean to sound angry, but I do.

"You were in my kitchen," he says.

This is not what I was expecting him to say.

"Yeah . . ."

I look at him closely, and I see sadness, fear, hope, all mixed together.

What is going on? And then I know.

Duh.

I am so stupid.

I put my hand on his arm. "Tell me about him," I say.

"Who? What?" he says angrily.

"Jake," I say softly, as warmly as I can. "Tell me about your brother."

"Did my mom tell you?"

So I'm right. "What?"

"That the boy in the pictures was my brother?"

"No. I guessed."

"Did she tell you anything?"

"No. We didn't talk about him at all."

"That's what she said. I didn't believe her."

I'm not completely getting this. "Can we talk, please?"

He shakes his head, seems like he's about to cry, and looks down at the floor.

Action, action, I say to myself, with a little less certainty. But when I look up at Jake again, he is looking at me, not at the floor.

"Come on, let's go sit outside."

He doesn't say anything.

"Come on."

Finally he nods, but I have to practically drag him down the hall.

We sit on the steps, off to one side, next to each other—not touching, but very close.

I sigh.

He sighs.

I take his hand. He doesn't let go.

We sit there for a while, just like that, looking at the street. His hand feels so good. He smells good, too. Lemony shampoo and a faint smell of chlorine.

After a few minutes, I look up at him. He's still staring off into space. I kiss him, very lightly, on the cheek.

He turns toward me and takes his other hand, the one not holding mine, and strokes my hair, kisses me lightly on the mouth. His lips feel chapped. He starts to kiss me harder, with his tongue exploring . . . I like it, I love it . . . but I pull away.

"Let's talk first," I say. "Then . . ."

He looks at me. Shakes his head, turns away.

I nod my head, firmly, and face him. We are still holding hands.

"I want to hear," I say. "Please."

His eyes well up, and then he starts talking.

"If we take *x* and assign it a value of 4.356 . . . ," Math Teacher drones.

We stayed outside for the whole period, and he told me what is behind his intense, sad eyes.

"The graph this shows us is . . ."

I can't believe what he has been through. And he didn't tell me everything, couldn't, just skimmed the surface, I'm sure. Why didn't I ever hear about this? Do my parents know?

All those years ago, after our kindergarten kiss, he and his parents moved south because his dad got assigned a residency down there. His mom was pregnant. They were happy, of course, and Jake was thrilled when he found out it was going to be a little brother. I always wanted a little sister, so I understand. I wonder why my parents never had another kid.

So Dr. Schmidt was out of town at a conference when Jake's mom went into labor, and he couldn't get back in time. Not that that would have made a difference, Jake told me emphatically. The baby's cord was wrapped around his neck and the doctor did an emergency C-section, but it was too late. Baby Jason was deprived of oxygen for so long that he came out severely mentally retarded.

Who even knew that stuff still happened?

Jake told me that his brother was adorable, and had he been who he was supposed to be, he would have been, Jake swears, a genius. "I could see it behind his clouded eyes every once in a while," Jake told me, "the glimmer of superintelligence." I don't know how he could tell, but I trust him.

Jake's parents were devastated, of course. Jake's mom wanted to move back here, but his dad felt it would be bad to leave, like a statement that it was the hospital's fault. So they stayed, and Mrs. Schmidt devoted herself to taking care of Jason. And Jake. Jake says that he barely remembers life before Jason, except our kiss, of course—

"How many people did the homework?" Math Teacher asks.

I do not raise my hand. I quickly look down so Math Teacher does not catch my eyes.

Jake told me his parents did their best to give him as much attention as Jason, though, of course, they couldn't possibly. His brother couldn't do anything at all. He had to have everything done for him. God, what kind of life did that leave for the rest of them? Poor Jake.

Two years ago Jason got meningitis. Jake's parents had already decided they wouldn't do "heroic" measures if Jason got sick, like you say you won't for old people. But when the time came and he was near death, they ignored all their plans and did everything they could to save him. He died anyway.

"I always thought it would be a relief," Jake told me. "But it wasn't. It was so horrible, so horribly sad. Our house was crazily *empty* without him."

After the funeral and *shivah,* they realized they couldn't stay there, in the house where Jason had lived, or in the community where they were known as Jason's family. So they moved back here.

"So that's it," he told me. "Now you know it all."

"I doubt it," I said. I reached up, ran my hand down his cheek, up through his hair, and down his back, his wonderful, strong back. And I gave him a good kiss.

"Rachel," he said. "Rachel, Rachel—"

"Rachel! Are you there?"

Oh no. That's not Jake. It's Math Teacher.

"Could you please repeat the question?" I say in my most polite Good Girl voice.

"I asked you which of these integers"—he is tapping the blackboard with his pointer—"would fill in this sequence properly?"

First I have to remember what an integer is. I think it's a number, and yeah, there are some numbers in a row on the left, with a space, and four other numbers on the right.

With a gut-wrenching epiphany I know what it feels like for Randy to look at a page filled with letters that seem like undecipherable scribbles. Not a single thing makes sense to him. From what Mrs. Glick said, he can recognize an *a* and an *n*, a *g*, *s*, and *t*, just as I can recognize those scribbles as numbers, but he can't put them together to read *angst*. Not that he'd know what that word means. Shit, he can't even put together *d* and *o* and *g* to make *dog* or *god*. As far as I can tell, *car* is the only word he recognizes besides his own name. I have got to help that poor guy learn to read. When I look up at the math board I see:

total gibberish.

I feel stupendously stupid. The tears start to well up in my eyes. I shake my head.

"Please come up to the board," Math Teacher says.

I walk up to the front of the room on shaky legs, as slowly as possible. Willing something to happen.

All of a sudden I hear noise in the hall.

"Action, action, we want action!" Is that in my head? No! The cheerleading squad is out there!

"Surprise pep rally!" someone yells, opening the door. I am a witch. "Everyone to the gym!" The whole class charges out.

Except for me and Math Teacher, both of us standing at the board. We look at each other.

"This sure is your lucky day," he says to me.

"Action, action, we want action," I say, rushing out into the hall to join the crowd.

CHAPTER 16

TO HAVE AND HAVE NOT

Every day this week, I talk to Alexis a little more at lunch. I've broken through her shell some. Now when I sit down she actually smiles and says hi. And on Thursday she sort of talks to me about this and that—nothing big, but she talks.

Maybe that's because at confirmation class on Wednesday night I sat in the back with her and Adam, doodling the whole time. We ignored the rabbi completely, creating the most gorgeous illicit drawings together. I don't know what I would have done if Jake had been there. But he's going to be missing a lot of confirmation class because of swim stuff. Said the rabbi was cool about it. "He is such a great guy."

I kept my mouth shut when he said that.

Trying to keep my mouth shut and my mind shut. If I don't think about His Holiness, I feel pretty good. Better. More like my old self.

And I've been thinking about Randy this whole week, looking forward to going back to Union, figuring out how I can reach him. Last night Mom said she was going to the mall. I asked her if I could come. I had an idea, as well as twenty dollars of saved-up money, and I hoped it would work. Luckily, the kids' store there was having a sale, and when I told Mom my idea, she gave me ten more dollars.

When I walk into the reading lab, Randy is sitting on the car pillow, of course. He's got a book in his lap, waiting for me. And I'm not even a second late!

"Hi, Randy." I wave. He jumps up, runs over, and gives me a hug. He's wearing the same bar mitzvah T-shirt.

"What's in that bag?" he asks me, pointing to the shopping bag from Kids' Korner. "Is it for me?"

Really? Can he read what it says? That little rascal.

"Why do you think it's for you?"

He looks at me shyly, shrugs. Now I feel bad. It's probably not that he can read the words. He sees the picture of the kids on the bag, and he's just hoping. . . .

"I'm not allowed to give you a present," I say, "but . . ." Now I'm worried that I won't be able to do what I want to do.

"What do you have there?" Mrs. Glick asks, walking toward us. Uh-oh.

"I hope this is OK," I say, talking really fast. "I was at the mall last night and I saw that the kids' store was having a sale so I got some T-shirts to have in the box for when, you know, kids spill or something on them-um-selves and I thought it would be a good idea and I—" Bluddity, bluddity, bluddity. Stop talking, Rachel.

I take the T-shirts out of the bag and show her. Each has at least one car on it. My favorite is covered with all different kinds of cars.

She looks at me, tilts her head, smiles, and says, "I guess

that's kosher. As long as they go in the box and are there for everyone."

I nod and put them in the box slowly, one at a time, so Randy can see what they are.

"Randy," Mrs. Glick says, "the shirt you're wearing has a hole in the back. It's getting colder out, so I think maybe you should pick out a shirt from the box to wear over it."

I'm about to say "or instead of," but I realize what she's thinking: don't make him give up one shirt for another. He needs both.

Randy dives into the box, looking at them carefully.

While he makes up his mind, I blurt out to Mrs. Glick, "What temple do you go to?"

"I don't belong to a temple," she says. "Not much into organized religion."

Wow, she seems so Jewish.

"Where do *you* go?" she asks me.

"Beth Am."

"Oh, Rabbi Cohn," she says. "I know him." Her voice is cold. She does not smile. One of the few people in the universe who doesn't love him?

How can I ask what I want to ask? But Randy is having none of this grown-up talk. He's tugging on my arm.

"Rachel, Rachel, can I have this one?" It's bright green with a yellow sports car on it. Not *my* favorite one, but that's OK.

"Sure. You want help?"

"I'm not a baby," he says.

He puts on the shirt, struggling a little, but then struts around showing off for the kids in the class. For a few seconds I see the real Randy, the one he is with his friends, not the Randy he is with older people he's trying to please, like me.

When we sit down to read, I think maybe he's following along, but I'm not sure.

Saturday afternoon, I shower with *kavanah.* It wouldn't be at all cool to show up at Jake's covered in Band-Aids. I shave my legs, my pits, even my toes (thank you, *Catalyst*, for that tip). Then I shampoo, condition, exfoliate, moisturize, pluck, dry, style, conceal, lip-line, eye-line, lash-lengthen, curl, gloss, blush, polish, and primp, primp, PRIMP as if my life depended on it.

Which I'm sure it doesn't.

It's not like we're going to be alone. I still think it's a little weird he asked me to come over for dinner on a Saturday night, instead of going to the movies or something. Maybe he's old-fashioned and thinks his parents need to approve of me?

In one way I'm relieved. I'm glad we're going to take things slowly. I'm not ready to be *alone* alone with him. As it is, my poor stomach is in knots. I have no idea what to wear. I want to look sexy for Jake, but proper for his parents.

I think about calling Alexis to ask her advice, but I don't. I can't chance a mood kill. In the end I decide to dress "modestly," as Grandma says.

A wrap dress, with a tank underneath so nothing shows. Leggings, ballet slippers. The dress is red, of course.

Mom comes up to see how I look, and she approves of the clothes. But when she looks at my face, she says, sweetly, "Wow. Makeup! You might want to take it down a notch." I look in the mirror. It is a little much. Mom dabs a tissue here and there.

"You're right, Mom, thanks. That's better."

"Perfect," she says.

Even *I* think I look good. My hair is smooth, just a little wavy at the ends, not at all frizzy. Maybe there really is a God.

I call Jake on the way over. He tells me to come around the back. In through the kitchen. I must have passed some test.

I still can't believe Mom said she didn't know about Jason when I asked her this morning. She'd better keep her promise not to say anything, in case they don't want people to know.

"Have fun," Mom says as I get out of the car. "Tell the Schmidts hello."

When I walk in, Jake is at the counter chopping. There's music playing, a song I don't know but I love right away. There is something cooking in a pan on the stove. It smells delicious.

Maybe this is not dinner with the parents.

"Hey," he says as I slip my shoes off and leave them by the door.

"You cooking?" I ask. Obviously he's cooking.

"Yup," he says, smiling.

"Can I help?"

"Nah. How about you sit over there, on the stool across from me, and keep me company."

I pull the stool up to the other side of the counter and sit down. He's mashing garlic and then cutting it.

"Why do you mash it first?"

"Lets out the flavor."

"How do you know that?"

"I used to watch a lot of cooking shows."

I don't say anything. I'm trying to picture this—Jake watching cooking shows.

"Back when my brother was alive, my mom didn't have time

to cook much, and neither did my dad, so once I was old enough, I kind of took over." He pauses, chops some more. "So I really love to cook. Do you think that's weird?"

"No. Not at all. I love it." It makes me love him, actually, right now, right here, for sure, but I won't say that. Not yet. He has to say it first. Man, what am I thinking? We haven't even made out yet. I mean, really made out. Like I really, really want to.

"What are you thinking about?" Jake asks. "You're turning bright red."

"Cooking?" I say, and laugh.

"Something hot," he says, and we look at each other. Smoldering looks. Smoking looks. Something smells like smoke.

"Oh shit, the oil is burning!" he says, and runs over to the stove. "Well, that's what I get for looking at you instead of at my pan. Got to start over."

He throws the pan into the sink and runs cold water over it. It sizzles, steams, and eventually cools off enough for him to wash it and put it back on the burner.

"OK then," he says, and grins at me.

"Could I get a drink of water?" I ask.

"Sure, there's cold in the fridge."

I look for the glasses. "There, above the microwave," Jake says, and I pour him one, too.

We clink and drink. He downs his in one long gulp, his Adam's apple bobbing. I have to look away; it is too sexy.

"So is it impolite to ask what you're making?" I say after I finish my glass.

"No! I'm making gemelli with olive oil and garlic. A side of Swiss chard sautéed also in garlic and olive oil, and a little balsamic vinegar. God, I hope you like garlic and olive oil. This meal is full of it!"

"I love garlic," I say. "And olive oil."

Jake looks at me, grins. "And if you like goat cheese, I'm going to add some of that to the Swiss chard, too."

Nobody in my house cooks like this. I'm not even sure I know what Swiss chard is. But it all smells delicious.

"I've made a small salad, and I thought we could have fresh berries with whipped cream for dessert. If we're still hungry."

"Where are your parents?" I ask. It may seem like a non sequitur, but it's not.

"They're out for dinner with friends. They won't be back for a few hours."

I get up from my stool and put my glass by the sink. I stand behind Jake and wrap my arms around him. My head reaches his shoulder blades and I lay it there, my cheek to his back, and breathe in his scent.

Dinner is scrumptious. We eat at the kitchen table, surrounded by photos of his family, but it is Jake and the food that overwhelm me. The pasta is amazing, and the Swiss chard is the most delicious green thing I have ever eaten.

He found what he called "the heel" of a bottle of red wine, poured us each some in wine glasses. He said his parents wouldn't mind. I think my parents would, but I drink it anyway. "To you," he said.

"To you," I say now. We each have a little bit left in our glasses. "This meal—God, Jake. Can I come here every night?"

He laughs. "Do you want some dessert?"

"I don't need dessert," I tell him.

"Good," he says. He stands up and takes my hand, leading me somewhere.

"What about the dishes?" I ask. My mother brought me up right, after all.

"I'll do them later," he says. We go into the living room, and he makes a show of turning on the TV and finding an old movie to watch. Turner Classics on Demand has an old Humphrey Bogart on.

"Have you seen this?" he asks.

"I don't think so," I say, but we start kissing before the movie even begins.

I've made out with boys before, but with Jake it is different. It's hot, but tender and sweet and, I don't know, meaningful. It feels right, so right that I don't feel scared or bad about myself, just happy, when his hand reaches up my dress and into my tank. I *want* him to touch me.

He is whispering how beautiful I am, telling me he loves my hair, my eyes, my arms, my legs, and I murmur things back to him, too.

Soon it feels urgent, I can't wait, and he starts to untie my dress, but then I

pull

way

back.

I am afraid. I am afraid if we don't stop, we could go all the way, and I am not ready for that.

"Jake, I—"

And he stops.

He looks at me, sees my face, sees *me*, and moves back a

little, too, though he is breathing hard. The kindness in his eyes overwhelms me. Well, maybe, maybe I will, we will, and I start to kiss him again and again and then all of a sudden—

I hear noises, voices.

His parents are home—and I don't have to make a decision.

We quickly put ourselves back together, sit facing the TV, feet on the floor, and Jake even turns on a lamp.

"Oh, it smells great in here!" Jake's dad booms. "Any left-overs?"

"We just came back from a huge meal, honey," his mother says, and by then they are in the living room.

"Ah! *To Have and Have Not*. Great flick," says Jake's dad. "That's the one where Bogart and Bacall fell in love, isn't it?"

"Hi, Rachel, how was dinner?" his mother says, jabbing his father with her elbow. I haven't seen her since the day I fled on my bike in the rain. I feel embarrassed (for so many reasons), but she gives me a warm smile.

Jake turns down the volume of the movie. I stand up.

"It was delicious, amazing," I say, and reach out my hand to shake his parents' hands. I pray I am all covered up and that I don't have a bite mark on my neck.

We shake, and then it is awkward.

"Let me put the movie on pause," Jake says.

"No, no, you go back to it," his dad says. "We're exhausted, we're going upstairs."

"Jake, you *will* do those dishes, won't you?" asks his mom.

"I'll do them," I say.

"They'll get done," Jake says. "Mood killer," he whispers to me as they walk upstairs.

"Maybe it's a good thing," I tell him. "If they don't want

grandchildren anytime soon." I laugh, but we both know it's not a total joke.

My mind is racing ahead to Planned Parenthood and birth control. Am I really ready for this? I don't think I am, but for some reason I smile.

So does he.

He grabs me into a big hug, but not a kiss, and says, "I don't trust them not to come downstairs again. I have to cool down."

"Let's do the dishes."

"What about the movie?"

"Doing dishes is safer than sitting on the couch."

"True, that."

I start clearing the table. I feel relieved that his parents came home. But also, I admit to myself, disappointed. I hope someday we'll . . . But I can't do that until I'm sure he, we . . . I don't want to feel used, or dirty. Wrong.

Will I ever get Crying Bride's sobs out of my head?

But this is Jake. Not *Him*.

We small-talk while we clean up, and then, after a few minutes of silence, Jake says, "I have to tell you something."

The tone of his voice—so serious—scares me. "What is it?"

He clears his throat. Looks at me nervously. "What you said about grandchildren—my parents want to have another child. They're adopting a little girl. From China. They've been talking about it pretty much ever since my brother died."

Phew. I don't know what I thought he was going to say, but I am so relieved. "Oh, that's wonderful! That will be so nice for you!"

Jake grunts. He doesn't say anything, just keeps scrubbing a frying pan.

"Isn't it? Wonderful, I mean?"

"No."

I wait.

"My whole life since he was born, it was all about Jason. Is it too much to ask that they focus on me my last few years at home?"

That's not what he said before, on the school steps. He said that he had a good childhood. Instead of sympathizing, I blurt out, "But if they wait much longer, until you've gone to college, won't they be too old?"

"They're too old already, really. My mom is forty-eight and my dad is fifty."

"So you don't think they should do it at all?"

"No, no I don't!" He slams down the pan and walks away. I don't know whether to follow him. I don't. I decide to wait for him to come back. I dry the frying pan and wash a bunch more dishes, put them in the dish rack. Finally, I hear the toilet flush and he comes back in. His eyes are red.

"I'm sorry. I know I seem like a selfish prick. I— It's just how I feel. I know they deserve happiness, but why can't they get it from me?"

"But you're going to be gone," I say softly. "And they won't have anyone left." Neither will my parents.

"You sound just like them," he says. The accusation and the bitterness in his voice go through my heart like a knife.

"I'm sorry," I say to him, reaching over to give him a hug. "I can't know how you feel."

"No, no you can't," he says, pulling away. "You will never know what it's been like for me."

Ouch. I *said* I couldn't know. I feel like stomping out, but instead I look at him; he's shaking.

I speak quietly. "You could try to tell me. I could try to understand—"

I trace a line down his spine with my finger. I feel him tense up, but I don't stop. I go up and down his back, first with my finger and then with the palm of my hand. It feels so good to touch him. I hope it feels good to him, too. After a while he leans on the counter, and he seems to be relaxing, giving in to me a little, and then I hear footsteps. It's his father walking into the kitchen.

I step back, take my hand away from Jake.

"God that meal was salty. Japanese. Delicious, but I'm dying for water."

I go to the cupboard, take out a glass, and hand it to Dr. Schmidt. He pours himself some water, finishes it in one gulp, and pours another. "I'm taking this up to your mom," he says to Jake.

Then to me: "Do you need a ride home?"

"No, my dad can get me."

"She was just about to call," Jake says.

I was?

CHAPTER 17

BLAH, BLAH, BLAH

We stand outside waiting for my dad. We don't talk, and it's awkward. But after a few minutes, Jake kisses me. A real kiss. A long, luscious kiss. Now I'm really confused. This guy is mercurial. I love that word. I love kissing him.

"I'm really sorry," he says. "I shouldn't have taken it out on you. I'm sorry."

"It's OK," I say, and I think it is. He's not perfect, but that's a good thing, right?

When my dad pulls up, Jake opens the car door for me and nods at my father.

"Good night, Jake," I say.

"Hi," says Dad as I get in.

"Hi."

We ride in silence, the radio on the jazz station Dad loves. Finally (it's been a whole two minutes), I can't stand it anymore. I text Jake.

`Thank you.`

He texts me right back.

`You're welcome.`

I text him again.

`It was delicious.`

He texts me.

`So were you.`

I sigh. Loudly.

Dad looks over at me. "What?" He has a hopeful look on his face, but his forehead is wrinkled.

"Nothing." I hold my phone to my heart.

Dad stops at a stop sign but does not go again, even though there is no one else at the intersection. He puts the car in park, turns off the ignition.

"You OK, Rachel?"

I look at him. "Yes. No. Yes. I don't know," I say, because it is the truth. Jake has me very confused.

"I love you, Rachel. And I know this is hard for you."

What is he talking about?

"But we'll work it out, I hope. Your mother and I. I mean, I know we will."

Oh.

"OK," I say. "Good."

Dad starts up the car and drives us home.

When I wake up in the morning, my first thought is not about Jake. It's about my father. In those few minutes between sleep and wake, when fragments of my dreams are still dusting my consciousness, the loud words in my head are: I blew it. I should have talked to Dad. I should have asked him about what was going on with him and Mom. Would he have told me the truth?

I get out of bed and keep thinking as I try on outfit after

outfit. I finally settle on tight jeans and a black top, kind of low-cut. I will definitely put a jacket on so Mom doesn't bother me.

I have never *dressed* for Sunday school before. I'm lucky if I even wash my face. Today I definitely wash it (still have some makeup on from last night), and I put on some eye liner and lip gloss. I want to make Jake wish he had not let me out of his arms last night.

I smile at myself in the mirror. The hair around my face is curling a little, but I kind of like that. I think I look pretty, beautiful maybe. Two days in a row! "Beauty comes from inside, Rachelleh," I hear Grandma's voice telling me.

I am ready to leave early enough to be able to walk. So I tell Mom and Dad I don't need a ride. They are sitting next to each other at the kitchen table, drinking coffee, looking OK, normal even.

"You look really pretty, Rachel," Mom says.

I can tell there is a question in her voice, but I ignore it. "Thanks." As a little gift, I am careful not to slam the door behind me as I leave.

What a beautiful morning! The sky is so blue, the air so crisp. It is one of those days that makes autumn my favorite season. I can't wait to see Jake.

Sunday classes aren't really mandatory, like the Wednesday night ones are—they are only every other week, and usually it's not the rabbi teaching, it's someone else. It used to be that I didn't want to go because it wouldn't be the rabbi teaching. Now, of course, I'm praying it's someone else, anyone else, so I don't have to sit in the same room as His Hypocrisy.

But today I don't really care, as long as I can see Jake. (I feel like this is a good sign—I am focusing on my own life, I am not obsessing about the stupid rabbi.) Maybe Jake and I will sit in the back and hold hands. Maybe we will walk home together, maybe we will . . .

But why should I be so lucky?

As I'm walking into the classroom, I get a text from Jake.

`My coach called. I have to lift weights for swimming. Sorry I won't be in class.`

And then the rabbi walks in. Damn.

He smiles when he sees me, and I pointedly do not smile at him.

I go sit in the back, next to Adam. Who is next to Alexis. The rabbi starts to talk.

This is what I hear of what the rabbi says:

Blah blah blah blah blah blah blah God blah blah blah blah blah *kavanah* blah blah blah blah blah *Torah* blah blah blah *tikkun olam* blah blah blah blah blah morality blah blah blah blah blah blah blah blah blah blah blah blah blah blah blah blah blah blah blah blah blah blah blah blah blah blah blah blah blah blah blah blah blah blah blah blah blah blah blah blah blah blah blah blah blah blah blah blah blah blah blah blah blah blah blah blah blah blah blah blah blah blah blah blah blah blah blah blah blah blah blah *kavanah* blah blah blah blah blah blah blah blah blah blah *tikkun olam* blah blah blah blah blah blah blah blah blah blah blah blah blah blah blah blah blah blah blah blah blah blah blah blah blah

blah blah blah blah blah blah blah blah blah blah blah blah blah
blah blah blah blah blah blah blah blah blah blah blah blah blah
blah do unto others blah blah blah blah blah blah blah blah blah
blah blah blah blah blah blah blah blah blah blah blah blah blah
blah blah blah blah blah blah blah blah blah blah blah blah blah
blah blah blah blah blah blah blah blah blah blah blah blah blah
blah blah blah blah blah blah blah blah blah blah blah blah blah
blah blah blah blah blah blah blah blah blah blah blah Rachel?
Rachel? blah blah intention and intentions, Rachel, blah blah
blah blah blah blah blah blah blah blah blah blah blah blah blah
blah blah blah blah blah blah blah blah blah blah blah blah blah
blah blah blah blah blah blah blah blah blah blah blah *keva* and
kavanah blah blah blah blah blah blah blah blah blah blah blah
blah blah blah blah blah blah blah blah blah blah blah blah blah
blah blah blah blah blah blah blah blah blah blah blah blah blah
blah blah blah blah blah blah blah intention blah blah blah blah
blah blah blah blah blah blah blah blah blah blah blah blah blah
blah blah blah blah blah blah blah blah blah blah blah blah blah
blah blah blah blah blah blah blah blah blah blah blah blah blah
blah blah blah *tikkun olam* blah blah blah blah blah blah blah
blah blah blah blah blah blah blah blah blah blah. blah blah
blah blah blah blah blah blah blah blah blah blah blah blah
blah blah.

Shalom.

When he's done saying whatever he was saying, the rabbi takes off his glasses. "Thanks, everyone. See you on Wednesday."

Then, "Rachel, come talk to me, please." I stop for a second, reflexively I guess, look at His Hypocrisy, feel sick to my stomach, turn around, and quickly leave before he calls me back.

I catch up to Alexis and Adam, who have bolted ahead, walking toward the Wawa.

"Alexis," I ask hopefully, "do you want to come over, or go shopping?"

She looks at her phone and says, "Can't. See ya," and starts to walk away.

"Hey, wait," says Adam. "I thought we were going to hang?"

"I have to go, sweetie," she says, turning around and looking at him. "But I'll talk to you later," she says definitely just to him, and saunters away.

The two of us watch Alexis go.

"Hey, Rachel," Adam says, putting his hand on my butt. "Wanna get high?"

"No thanks," I say. Why does it feel good to have *his* hand on my butt? I leave. Fast.

CHAPTER 18

KISSING ELEPHANTS II

"And then, on the runway, with everyone looking—like, billions of people—she tripped on that stupid dress!" says Kendra.

"Fell on her face!" Marissa laughs.

"I bet she was high on something!"

"Her ego," snarks Alexis.

Vintage Alexis. We all laugh, even me, which is weird because I don't watch this show, never will. So not into it. I am a stranger in a strange land.

At that moment Jake appears beside me, as if God is reassuring me, *You are not alone*.

"I'm on a bathroom pass from French," he says.

He bends down, moves my hair away, and whispers into my ear, his lips lightly touching my skin. "So will you walk home with me today? I mean partway—I have to go to swim practice."

I have to swallow before I can speak. "Sure," I tell him as nonchalantly as possible. I was going to stay after school and work on Yearbook, that's what I told Mom, but Jake trumps Yearbook any day.

"Great," he says, and turns to leave. But then he moves

closer, puts his hand on my shoulder, and whispers into my ear again, making me crazy. "See you later."

I turn my head. I want to pull him to me, give him a long, deep kiss. Right there.

But of course I don't.

I just nod, and savor the feeling of his hand on my shoulder and his lips on my ear and his fingers in my hair. I put my own hand on my shoulder, where his was, as I watch him walk away.

"What was *that?*" Alexis asks me. The look on her face is—what? Disapproval? Disdain? Envy? I can't read her anymore.

I smile slightly but say nothing. I don't want her to ruin this.

Before she can ask more, I stand up, dump my tray, and leave.

I have no idea what happens in any of my classes for the rest of the day. All I can think is: Jake.

At final bell I go to the nurse. I ask her for a toothbrush and toothpaste, and she gives me them, no questions asked. I put her near the top of my list of Decent Human Beings.

Jake is waiting for me in front of the building, near where we sat the day he told me about his brother. As soon as we get a block away, he pulls me behind a tree and kisses me.

Our first kiss is bumpy—literally. We bang noses and don't quite get our mouths together. I am about to say something funny, but he takes my face in his hands and puts his mouth on mine, and it's amazing how good this feels. It's even better than Saturday night.

I love his lips, the scratchiness of his cheeks and chin, his hands in my hair. . . . I run my hands up and down his back, which makes me think of our dinner, which makes me think, for some reason, of our first time kissing on that other walk home, and I think of how we talked about elephants and we are elephants kissing, and I pull back and look at him. "What?" he says. He looks wary even though I'm smiling.

"Nothing," I say, and start to kiss him again.

"No, what?" he says, pulling away. "What is it?" Boy is he insistent.

"Elephants," I say, "kissing elephants." He grins a big grin, and I know he gets it.

"Oh, Rachel," he whispers, "you are so beautiful and smart and funny and so . . ." and he kisses me on my neck and on my ear, the same ear that he whispered into before, and

I really do think I am in love with him.

After a while, I hear a shout and then more shouts and I realize that even though I feel like we are alone in the world, Jake and I actually are standing in a tiny grove of trees right next to a playground. There are little kids on the swings, in the sandbox, on the sliding board. I'm sure they can see us. I don't think they *should* see us, especially since Jake now has his hand up my shirt, and I seem to have my hand in his back pocket, and we are both breathing hard.

I stop kissing him, and I pull out my hand.

"Can we walk a little?"

He nods. We start walking, holding hands, and are quiet for about a block. I assume we're both trying to cool down a little when he says, "I still feel bad about the other night. I'm sorry I was such an ass about my potential little sister."

"No, *I'm* sorry," I say. "I should have been more sensitive."

"No, no, it was *me*. You were perfect that night. You *are* perfect," he says, and then he stops and he kisses me again, first gently, and then hard, urgent, until he pulls away, leaving me wanting more.

This is how the rest of the walk goes: we walk a block, talk a little, then one of us stops, grabs the other one, we kiss passionately, and then we walk on. (He does most of the grabbing, but I try to keep up.)

I wish I could get home like this every day: Walk, talk, stop, kiss. Walk, talk, stop, kiss. If I were a songwriter, I'd write a love song with that title: "Walk, Talk, Stop, Kiss." Any doubts I have about Jake, like the kind of weird way he sometimes says things—"potential little sister"—or the way he can get moody, would not be in the song.

Or maybe those things should be in a love song, because nobody is perfect, even if he thinks I am.

I am going to stop overthinking this and let myself be happy.

Because I *am* happy. So happy.

Because of Jake. Because of who I am with Jake. Because of the world with Jake in it.

The more we kiss, the happier I am. Screw the rabbi. Screw my parents. Screw Alexis. Life is good. Better than good.

Even after we finally say good-bye and go our separate ways, I feel like I am flying, I feel like I could really fly . . . but I don't want to get home too quickly, I don't want to break the spell. And because it's late in the afternoon now, one or both of them could be there, and they could be fighting—or worse, not talking to each other.

Mom's not expecting me for at least another half an hour anyway. So I put on my love-song playlist and walk really slowly, eating a granola bar, thinking about Jake and those kisses, wondering if I will be going to Planned Parenthood soon. The thought makes me happy and scared. Excited. Alive.

I prolong the walk home, kicking rock after rock until I lose each one in the gutter and then find another so that a walk that shouldn't take even fifteen minutes takes much longer.

But not long enough.

I should get home too late to see them at the top of the driveway leaning against his big black SUV, hip to hip, his hand reaching up to the strand of her hair that's hiding her left eye. Too late to see her smile and hear the ripple of her laughter as his other hand reaches over and brushes away hair that is hiding nothing.

I am not too late for any of this. I see it all. But I do not trust it, or trust my gut, until I see him pull her face to his and

I stop dead in my last stone kick

to see the rabbi kiss my mother and my mother kiss him back.

CHAPTER 19

THE PUNCH LINE

I run.

I run fast and I run hard. Away from home, away from school, away from everything.

Feel punched in the gut. And still I run. Run through the twisted knots of pain.

I am not a runner. And these sneakers are not made for running.

They're made for walking slowly home, kissing your boyfriend. They're not made for running like hell because you just saw your mother making out with the rabbi.

I run and run, my messenger bag bouncing, thwacking me on my back, my hip, my stomach, pretty much every step of the way.

What the hell?

Right in our driveway.

She thought I'd be home later.

But—

What if Dad had come home early?

What if

Dad had

pulled up and

had seen them?

Maybe he did.

Good.

Bad.

I don't know which.

My body says stop running it hurts I hurt my chest hurts

But I keep going.

Did they see me?

I doubt it. I was at the bottom, and there's that curve.

But do I care?

Do I hope they saw me?

Am I going to tell Mom I saw?

Tell Dad?

Where am I going?

Am I going to run away from home?

Run until I die?

My heart is pounding in my chest, and I can barely catch my breath, but I do

not stop

running.

I don't care what happens to me. Let my heart burst in my chest, too. I don't care.

I really fucking don't.

I look up at where I am.

Of course.

My feet have taken me to the only person in my family I can turn to, hopeless as it may be. Maybe she will be good today.

Maybe it will be

one
of her
I. Am. Going. To. Die.
good days.
Maybe.

I am here not a moment too soon. I can barely breathe. There are invisible nails digging into my feet, the bottom, the sides. Are my toes broken? Everything hurts. My back, my side, my chest, my legs, my head.

I thought I was in decent shape. I had no idea.

About anything.

I *have* no idea.

She can't see me like this, sweaty, panting. Tears running down my face. I didn't even know I was crying.

I sit down in front of her door. Take off my shoes. There is blood all over my feet. God, was it these same feet that were walking with Jake? Just—was that today?—minutes ago?

I lean back against the door, try to breathe normally. Yeah, right.

Reach into my bag and find a tissue. Wipe my face. Wipe the blood off my feet. It's not as bad as I first thought, two blisters and a broken toenail. They are throbbing, but no permanent damage has been done. To my feet.

I keep trying to get a sense of humor about this, but I can't find the damn joke. Must be here somewhere. A rabbi and a mother walk into a bar . . . no, onto a driveway. . . .

Not funny. Not even slightly.

What's the punch line?

• • •

I am breathing about as normally as I ever will. But I hurt too much to get up.

Can't reach the bell, so I knock loudly on her door. No answer. I knock really loudly and call out, "Grandma! It's Rachel," but nothing.

What am I thinking? The woman can't hear me if I'm in the next room—hell, if I'm in the same room—why should she hear this? But I can't stand up.

I call her. I hear Grandma's phone ring and ring inside her apartment. Clicks to her voicemail. I don't leave a message. Maybe she is in the bathroom. I wait five minutes, or an hour—I have no idea how long. I close my eyes tight, trying to get that image of my mother and the rabbi kissing out of my head, but it is all that is there. I call again. No answer.

I have a key. I should stand up and open the door. But it is not only my aching body that stops me. What if she's lying there on the floor?

Bleeding.

Dead.

Do I really want to go in and see that?

What could be worse than seeing my mother kiss the rabbi? Seeing my grandmother lying dead on the floor.

I call again. Nothing.

I'd better go in there.

I could save her life.

What could be worse than seeing my grandmother dead? Knowing I could have saved her and didn't.

I start to stand up, and then I see her.

She is not answering her phone because she is not inside. She is walking down the road in her bathrobe and slippers. Carrying her purse, and—what is that?—the cordless phone from her living room. Oh, Grandma.

Her hair is a mess, sticking out all over. My grandma, who never leaves her house without makeup, her "face" she calls it.

She's crying. She walks past her door. She doesn't see me.

I try not to sob as I hobble over to her in my bare feet. The cold street actually feels good, and I concentrate on that. She's stopped walking. She is staring at the ground. When I reach her, her head is bent, and she is weeping softly.

"Grandma," I whisper, touching her gently on the shoulder. She doesn't look up.

"Grandma," I say a little louder.

She looks up at me and says, "I can't find my husband. Where is my husband?"

My heart is aching. "Grandma, it's me, Rachel."

"Who? I don't know you! Where is my husband? What have you people done with my husband?"

"I'm Rachel, Grandma," I say, choking up, feeling that granola bar rise in my throat. "Grandpa is not here anymore, Grandma. Grandpa died."

Grandma looks at me, furious. "What are you saying?" she yells.

Hello, God? Do you hear me? I can't take this.

I reach up and touch her on the shoulder, the tears now freely running down my cheeks. "Shhhh, shh," I say, just like she used to say to me when I was little. "Shh, shh, it will be OK."

She looks at me—sees me, I think.

But she pushes my hand away. "Go away. I don't know you."

"I'm your granddaughter . . . ," I manage, dizzy, the nausea threatening.

"Go to hell," says my sweet grandma. "Go to hell," she yells, "you stupid, lying BITCH."

I can't hold it in anymore.

The puke starts to come out, and I jump back quickly so I won't hit Grandma, and instead of throwing up on her, I throw up on my bare feet.

CHAPTER 20

PARTY ANIMAL

Grandma starts to howl when she realizes who I am.

"Oh, Rachel, Rachel!" she cries. "Help me!"

I try to reassure her as I call Dad, not Mom, because, well, I have no idea what she's doing at this minute. Kissing the rabbi? Or more? God.

"I'll be right over," Dad says calmly. "Try to get her inside."

Which I do, with the help of Mrs. Philips, who magically materializes by my side with paper towels and a kind voice. I will love her forever. She asks no questions, just cleans me up and gets Grandma into the apartment. She pours me some ginger ale, makes Grandma a cup of instant decaf, chitchatting about absolutely nothing, calming us both down.

Maybe there are honestly good people in the world. Maybe there are.

And then my mother the slut walks in.

Dad is behind her.

"Here I am, Mother," she says, and goes right over to Grandma, soothing, caring, but all I see is the image of her kissing the rabbi.

For the next hour or so that image is overlaid on everything, the lens I see it all through: Dad's concerned face, his hand gently on Mom's back, Mrs. Philips quietly leaving, Grandma sobbing again, Mom so upset, Dad trying to figure out why my feet are torn up.

My mother and I do not exchange more than a word.

She stays with Grandma for the night, and Dad drives me home. I want to tell him. Or do I? I could be the one who ends their marriage. How could I do that?

I debate this for a minute and then fall into a deep sleep even though it's a ten-minute drive.

"Hungry?" Dad asks as he helps me out of the car.

"No," I say. I crawl up the stairs and right into bed, dirty, sweaty, pukey, bloody.

Sleep until morning.

I want to skip school, but the thought of staying home is not appealing either, so I shower and go. Maybe I will see Jake. I read his text first thing this morning:

`Rachel, beautiful Rachel.`

After one class, I know it's not happening.

Pleading, I get the nurse to let me sleep on her cot. I tell her about my grandma and that my mother is too busy taking care of her to come get me. I text with Jake a little: he's off to another swim meet. He'll be back tomorrow night, maybe, or Sunday.

`So much to tell you,`

I write.

`Want to hear everything you have to say,`

he answers.

The nurse lets me stay until lunch and then kicks me out. I make it through the rest of my classes, and then, since it's Friday, I drag myself to Union and to Randy.

When I get there, I see Mrs. Glick huddled in the corner with Randy and Mrs. Washington. Randy is crying. When he sees me, he comes running, and I take him into a big hug.

Mrs. Glick tells me over his head that his grandmother, the person he lives with because his mom is in jail and he's got no dad, was rushed to the hospital last night. That's all they know. A neighbor brought him to school and told them.

I don't know what to do. What can I do? I take Randy to the car pillow, and he just cries into my shoulder. Eventually he falls asleep. Just before the end of class, the principal comes into the room.

"Randy," she says, and I gently wake him up. "There's someone here to take you home."

"Who?" says Randy.

"A cousin of your mom's."

Randy shrugs and gets up.

I want to yell, Wait, I'll take him home! He can't go with someone he doesn't know! But of course I don't know if he doesn't know the cousin; and of course I can't take him home.

There's nothing I can do.

Mrs. Glick speaks up, though. "Can I go up with you?"

The principal nods. "Of course," she says, and they leave.

I wonder if I'll ever see Randy again.

At dinner, which is takeout Chinese, something we never do on Friday night, Mom tells Dad and me what she and Uncle Joe have decided to do about Grandma. They're putting her on anti-anxiety pills. And after consulting with doctors, they are letting her stay at home, with a full-time aide, who will sleep on the couch at night.

Like Dad.

Through Mom's talking I keep thinking about what I saw. Mom and the rabbi. I can't believe she's having an affair with him. Is she? How could she? He's gross. So gross.

At midnight I get up to snoop. I tiptoe into Mom's den.

I check her phone. There are numbers I don't recognize, and when I Google them, most of them are doctors or nursing homes. One that is unlisted.

I look over caller ID on our landline. Nothing. No calls from the temple, which is kind of weird. Wouldn't Mom have told him what is going on? Wouldn't he call to check up on Grandma?

I try to log on to her email account. She's changed her password. It used to be Rachel-1. I try all her usual passwords. Nothing works.

Why would my mother change her password?

I go into her bedroom, shake her awake, demand an answer. Yeah, in my dreams.

What I really do is tiptoe into the kitchen. I'm starving.

"Hey," Dad calls out to me from the couch. "Can't sleep?"

"No," I say.

"Me neither," he says.

He pads into the kitchen, and the two of us sit at the table and eat heaping bowls of cereal topped with Mom's granola.

It's like one of those sweet father-daughter scenes in a movie, only we don't talk. I sit there and think about my mother cheating on my dad with the rabbi. God knows what my dad is thinking about.

Saturday afternoon, Alexis calls and tells me there's a party. Do I want to go? When I say maybe, she says, "Can your parents give us a ride? My mom's busy."

Oh. Yup. And so I go.

We've been here ten minutes and she's ditched me already. I'm by the food. She's across the room, flirting with three boys *and* two girls around the pool table. I'm not a prude, but . . . yes I am. So what am I going to do at this party? I don't want to be here. Unless Jake comes.

Half of me wants to go home. The other half is waiting for Jake. (Which half, Rachel?) When I last texted him, he said he might be back from his swim meet in time.

`Not my kind of party,` he wrote. `But I'll try.`

Not my kind of party either. I don't really even know the kid whose house it is. Dennis Kaufman. He's a year older than we are. He's kind of a loser and a druggie. But my parents know his parents, so Mom didn't put up a fuss.

She hardly said good-bye when I left. What is going to happen—? No, I will not go there. I will not go anywhere but here. Where I am. This is my *kavanah* of the evening: be here now. Be HERE. I'm going to make it my intention. Live in the moment. Live for the moment.

What will that mean, here in Dennis Kaufman's basement?

His house is a typical big suburban banana split, as Dad calls them, with rooms upon rooms. The basement is full of new furniture and old leftover furniture. There are, like, three couches, a couple of club chairs, lots of pillows, lots of carpet . . . lots of places to make out. I am beginning to see why Alexis said this is a great place for a party.

Who is she hoping to get with? Assuming she's not being faithful to Mitch.

"Hey, Raebee," she says to me now. Holding out a plate of brownies. "These are pot brownies. Paul made them with his sister." She nods at some kid from school who I vaguely know. He's a senior, I think. She takes two and puts the plate on the table.

Should I take one? I don't really want to get stoned. But I kind of do. I mean, why not? It might make the night more fun.

What the hell? I take one, gobble it down.

Try to make conversation.

"Did you ever get new jeans?"

"No," she says.

"Morrison's is having a sale. Wanna go?"

"Maybe," she says, and walks away. I eat another brownie.

A few kids come over, take brownies. "How's it going?" they say.

"How's it going?" I say.

Scintillating.

I should leave. But what if Jake comes? I want to be with him, talk with him, touch him, kiss him, have him hold me. I will feel so much better when his arms are around me. I pull out my phone to text him when I hear a shout from the pool table.

Adam won. They're starting a new game and he's racking up the balls.

He looks so good tonight. He's wearing a black T-shirt and black jeans. His hair is shorter than it's been in a while, styled in that mussed-up way. I see his muscles through his T-shirt as he hits ball after ball. I jump a little bit with each crack as the ball goes into its hole. He's very good. So sure of himself. So in control.

I lean up against the wall, watch Adam. It's OK to watch him. Just watch. A girl can enjoy, right?

I don't let myself think about the fact that he's the rabbi's son. That would ruin everything. OK, it just did.

I quickly text Jake and say,

`You coming?`

I check my phone every two seconds for an answer. Nothing.

Meanwhile, Adam is shooting me looks. He knows I'm watching him. What am I doing? Am I crazy? I like *Jake*. And Adam is the fucking rabbi's son, for God's sake. My choice of inner-thought words cracks me up, and I laugh out loud.

Oh shit, stoned again. Which makes me laugh for some reason. Do I laugh a lot always, or only when I'm stoned?

Adam looks up at me and grins his lopsided half smile he has that all of a sudden I realize means I like you, but I'm too cool to give you a whole smile. You could earn a whole smile, though. . . .

Jake, you'd better get here fast.

The pool game ends. Adam won again, of course. Got that last ball right in the pocket.

Someone puts on soft music and turns the lights low. Adam walks over. He digs his hand into the bowl of pretzel M&M's.

"Hey," he says to me.

"Hey," I say back.

"What's up?" he says after he's eaten a handful of the M&M's, making that, somehow, sexy. Maybe I should just be HERE now.

"Not much."

He leans into me a little, which for some crazy reason sends an electric charge through me.

My mind flashes to something I just learned in biology class: there are many birds that *seem* to be monogamous, that scientists have thought for years were monogamous, but they actually cheat.

Adam whispers in my ear.

I don't hear what he says, but I get chills.

I pull back.

"What?" I ask.

"Huh?"

"I didn't hear what you said," I say, a little too loudly.

He pulls me to him and whispers in my ear again, loudly enough for me to hear him this time. "You look sexy tonight."

I do?

I changed a million times and finally settled on jeans and a black top, the kind with spaghetti straps. I have a red bra on underneath. I knew my mother would throw a fit, so I threw another shirt, red, pretty see-through, on top of it all. You can see everything: the bra, the black shirt, the red shirt on top. I don't think I look sexy. I think I look like a clothing ad gone wrong.

But Adam thinks I look sexy. I don't *feel* sexy.

Well, maybe a little. The way he's looking at me I do. The way he's touching me very slightly with his body as we stand side to side leaning against the wall.

I see Alexis on the other side of the room. I sure don't want to piss her off.

"Aren't you going to hang with Alexis tonight?" I ask Adam at the same time I motion Alexis to come over.

But Adam leans into me ~~the way I saw his father lean into my mother~~, his left hip to my right hip, his left arm is tracing a line up and down my neck, distracting me, distracting me—

"I'm hanging with you," he says, his voice low and husky.

Jake? I pray silently. Walk down those steps now. Save me from myself. Lex? Come over, please.

Alexis giggles, and we both watch her go into another room with that kid Paul, their arms around each other. I feel Adam tense up, and I don't know if it's because he likes Alexis. Or maybe because he likes Paul. Who knows? Or is he jealous that they are getting action and he's not? Yet. Yet? Why did I think that?

I pull myself straight and think of Jake. I think of right and wrong. I think of who I am and what I believe. I don't actually feel stoned. Not like last time. But maybe I am. I should eat something. Jake would tell me to eat something. I reach over and grab a handful of potato chips, which taste really, really good. Salt and fat; you can't beat that.

I move away from Adam, take more food.

Whatever Alexis and Paul are going to do, even if it is make out, even if it's make a *baby*, it doesn't mean it's all right for me to do something with Adam. Just because my mother is a slut . . .

But now Adam's next to me again, playing with my hair.

Jake? Where are you?

Adam's whispering in my ear and I can't hear all the words, but I hear "sit down" and "rub your back," and before I can say

"Jacob Schmidt" three times fast, I am in a dark corner with Adam, on a few overstuffed pillows, and he's rubbing my back and kissing my neck and it feels soooo good.

After a while, I turn to say something to him, to try to take this down a notch, to make some conversation, but he doesn't wait for me to talk. He covers my lips with his and his tongue is in my mouth and even though it's not Jake, he's not Jake, and his kisses are too wet and sloppy, I still get tingles from the way he is touching me, where he is touching me, and it's not like it was with Jake at all, with Jake I felt something in my heart, my brain, and my body, but this is only about my body, the way my body feels. I don't really even like Adam, sometimes I even hate him, but he makes my body feel so good and my last thought before losing all *kavanah* is: I really hope Jake doesn't come here tonight. And I reach into my pocket and turn off my phone.

Eventually we find another room. There is a mattress on the floor. I think there might be another couple in here, somewhere, but I don't care. I am beyond caring. Adam is touching me all over. I want to touch him all over. His shirt is off. My shirt is off. So is my bra. I don't care about anyone or anything right now.

He moves my hand to his pants.

"Touch me," he says.

I put my hand there.

"Rub," he says to me softly.

I rub.

"I have a condom," he whispers, and I hear it rustling in his hand.

I

freak.

I can't go there. Not now. Not with him. Not with *him*. Not with *Adam*.

God, what was I doing? What was I thinking?

He's kissing me hard and holding my head with one hand and unwrapping the condom with the other, spreading my legs with his knee.

"No!" I say.

"Oh yes!" he says in a husky voice. "Yes, Rachel, yes . . ."

NO!

I jump up, knocking my elbow in his face.

"Ow!" he yelps. "Fuck!"

"I'm sorry, I'm sorry. I didn't mean to—but I can't!"

I grab my shirt, my bra and, covering my boobs, run out of the room. I open the first door I see, dash in, and *whack!* run right into something hard. With my head.

OW! Fuck!

I search in the dark for a light switch, tears streaming down my face from the pain. I feel shelves, boxes. . . . This is *not* a bathroom.

Finally I find a string and pull it. I'm in a closet.

Hit my head on that tall bureau. On the corner. I feel blood.

I start to get hysterical, but I can't do that. I can't. Have to get out of here and find a bathroom. I breathe deeply. Please, Rachel, calm down. Please. Calm down. After a few minutes I open the door, look up and down the hall. I don't see anyone. I put on my black top. Oh no. I must have left my red shirt in the other room, with Adam. Great.

I stuff my bra in the back pocket of my jeans and walk down the hall, opening door after door until I find a bathroom.

Above the sink is an old and dirty mirror. I take some toilet paper, wipe it off.

I see someone who looks like me, but not. I am a horror show. My forehead is bleeding. I have red marks all over my neck, and on my tiptoes I can see some on my chest, too. My nipples hurt. I wanted every touch, every suck, and it sure didn't hurt then, but now . . .

I keep looking at myself in the mirror until I can't stand it anymore. Beauty comes from the inside? So does ugliness, Rachel.

I take some more toilet paper and wet it a little, clean up my forehead. It's only a scratch. No trip to the emergency room, thank goodness. I can just see trying to explain this to my parents. I put pressure on to stop the bleeding. Dad taught me to do that.

Dad. Shit. Poor Dad.

I am my mother's daughter.

Jake. Oh Jake. Oh God. I pray he didn't come. I pray Adam has not walked out into the room, waving my shirt above his head in victory, for Jake and all to see. Oh please, God, no. I pray. I pray with as much *kavanah* as I've got.

I take the toilet paper away. The bleeding has stopped. For once I'm glad my hair is a curly, frizzy mess. I move a mop over to cover the scratch, smooth it out with my fingers. Good enough.

I hide in the bathroom for as long as I can. No one comes looking for me. Not Alexis, of course. Not Adam. I hear laughter. I hear music. I have got to get out of here. I turn my phone back on. Shit, I have a text from Jake. I don't read it. I don't want to know. I call home. I need to get out of here. No answer. No answer? Where are they?

I get up, throw water on my face. Don't look in the mirror. I breathe deeply.

My phone vibrates. Another text. I ignore it. Denial is a river in Egypt. Hardy har har. I have to get out of here without talking to anyone.

I walk out into the main room, my head down. Don't stop, keep walking. I can't help but look, and out of the corner of my eye I see boys at the pool table. They're laughing. Jake's there.

Of course he is.

Oh, Jake. Oh, me.

Guess I didn't pray with enough fucking *intention*.

I walk quickly up the steps and get the hell out of this house.

I call home again. It rings five times. Finally Mom picks up.

"I need a ride."

"Really? Now?" says Mom. "It's so early."

"Really," I say. "Please."

"OK," she says, and hangs up quickly.

And then I wait. I wait. I wait in the cold night air.

I wait and wait. Where's Dad? I don't want to be alone with my thoughts. And my shivers. It is really cold outside. And I only have on my little black top. "A bit of a nip in the air," I say to myself, out loud. "A bit of a nip."

Nip. Bite. Who knew that biting could be such a thing in sex?

For the first time I understand how a girl could be stupid

enough to go all the way and get pregnant with someone she doesn't love. I just had crazy almost sex with a boy I don't even like most of the time.

"You're so hot." Adam said that to me as he put his hand—no, I won't go there, can't go there. I shake it off.

Shake, shake, shake.

I'm still shaking when Dad's car pulls up. I go to open the front passenger door, but Mom's sitting there.

I climb into the backseat and mumble, "Hi."

Mom half turns around and says, "How was the party?" but it's a distracted question, I can tell. Her hand is on Dad's thigh. I expect her to yell at me about how little I'm wearing, but she doesn't say anything.

I look at them more closely. Mom's hair is a mess. Dad is stroking Mom's neck.

WTF?

"Rachel?" Mom says.

"What?" I snap.

"How was the party?" she snaps back.

"Fine," I say.

"Isn't it early to be coming home?" Dad says, stepping on the gas.

"I guess," I say. Not early enough.

"And we thought Alexis's mom would be picking up, since I drove you here," he says, annoyed.

I don't say anything. I don't have to. I can tell all they want to do is get back home and get rid of me.

Dad pulls into the driveway and I run into the house. Panda is sleeping on the living room couch. "Panda Cat," I say, and pick her up gently, cradling her in my arms so she won't jump away.

I run upstairs to my bedroom, close the door, and turn on some music nice and loud. Then I burrow under the covers with my cat and try to sleep until I'm twenty.

CHAPTER 21

A LITTLE BOMB

Morrison's department store is crowded with Christmas shoppers.

Alexis and I are not Christmas shoppers or even Hanukkah shoppers.

We are two teenage girls pretending to be friends.

This is what I think as we make our way through the men's department. We have come to Morrison's together dozens of times; since we turned eleven our parents have let us ride the bus alone. We look like we are still those friends. Alexis's mom, Ginny, used to tell us that when you are feeling sad, you smile until your inside catches up with your outside. So maybe if we act like friends, we'll be friends again.

But later, in the dressing room, I realize we are way beyond that. I snap shut these jeans I really like and Alexis says, "Those are too small for you. Unless you're going for the 'fat slut' look. Which—I guess . . ."

She gives me a withering look, a look I have only seen on her face once or twice, directed at her mother. When she was hating her.

We have gone into a different zone.

The zone of destruction. But why?

I want to say, Yeah, that's exactly the look I'm going for, how'd you know?

I should say this in as sarcastic a tone as I can manage. But I'd cry if I opened my mouth. I have an awful feeling this is just the beginning of her attack.

I take off the jeans and throw them onto the floor. I am too tired. Tired of betrayal. Tired of idols crashing to the ground. Tired of disappointment. Tired of myself.

I can't believe I did that last night. What is the matter with me?

I forced myself to look at Jake's texts before I got out of bed this morning.

The first one said,

`I'll be right there. Can't wait to see you.`

The second one:

`I'm here. Where ARE you?`

Good question. I am here! I could have said. If only . . .

There was a third text from Jake:

`I'm leaving.`

How am I ever going to explain to him why I did what I did?

"By the way," Alexis says as we leave the dressing room to look for the same jeans in the next size up, "those weren't pot brownies. Those guys kept the pot ones all to themselves."

Wait a minute. What?

I did that with Adam and I wasn't even stoned? I felt stoned. Sort of. But not really. Not actually stoned, now that I think about it. I am an even worse person than I thought. Oh, Jake.

"Here they are, in a bigger size," Alexis says loudly, cheerfully, and drags me back into the dressing room.

I unzip my pants, think of Adam unzipping my pants last night, how we almost—

"Oh, and too bad you left early last night," Alexis says.

I don't answer. I put on the new jeans, zip them up easily. Turn, look at myself sideways in the mirror. Not bad.

"Don't you want to know why?"

I shake my head. I don't. I really don't.

Nah. These jeans are too big. I take them off. I'm going to buy the other ones. I grab them and leave the dressing room. Maybe they're too tight. But I don't care. What the hell. My hand shakes as I pay for them, Alexis hovering nearby. Why doesn't she just leave?

As we are riding the escalator down to the first floor, she turns to me.

"Oh. Yeah, so," she says, yawning, "I hung out with Jake after you left the party. Told him you slept with Adam."

"You told Jake that? Why would you tell him that? Why would you do that to me?"

Alexis shakes her head. "Truth hurts, doesn't it?"

"Well it's not the truth, anyway, Alexis! I did not sleep with Adam!" I hiss.

"Yeah, not much *sleeping* going on," she says.

"I did *not*," I say again. But what's the use? I can never prove it.

But why would she tell him?

We get off that escalator, walk around to the next one.

"Oh, and, Raebee—" She looks at me, makes sure I'm looking at her. "Your Jake is a really good kisser. I wouldn't have thought so, but he *is*."

"What are you talking about?" I ask, my heart sinking into the floor.

"We hooked up."

"No way!" I shout at her. She's lying!

"What, you think I'm such a dog he wouldn't want to fool around with me? That you're so much better—?"

"NO! He likes *me*! Why would he do that with you?" Even as I say it, I hear the irony. "Why would *he* do that?" People passing us on the up escalator look at me and then look away.

She shrugs. "Um, gee, I don't know, Ms. Perfect. What do *you* think?"

"No way! There is no way Jake would have done *that* with you."

"Oh, way," she says to me in her best sexy voice. "How could he resist me?"

"And you, Alexis, how could you . . . do that?" To me.

She looks past me, shrugs. "Me? Bored." Then she looks straight into my eyes. "He's got such a great back, doesn't he? So strong, so hard . . ."

She gets off the escalator before me. I have to hold on really tight so I don't fall off. Alexis turns around and gives me a look that says, I *wanted* to hurt you, and I'm glad I did. But what her mouth says is "Let's look at jewelry," as if nothing just happened.

I follow her.

I follow her because I want

to

kill

her.

I have never hated anybody so much in my whole life. I don't think I've ever actually hated anyone before. Not even His Holiness.

She goes to a jewelry counter, and while she's diddling with this and that, I force myself to stare at her. Alexis. My best friend. The only best friend I've ever had.

She seduced Jake. She told him I slept with Adam. As if what I did wasn't bad enough, she made it so much worse. I was going to talk to Jake, explain, and now . . .

She slept with him? He slept with her?

Rage courses through me, venom in my veins.

The saleslady, a tight-lipped, tight-assed, tinted-haired old lady—MRS. ELLIOT, YOUR MORRISON'S FRIEND, it says on her nametag—is fiddling with her keys to find the right one to open up the locked case so Alexis can look at an expensive watch (as if she is really going to buy a Movado).

Jake's beautiful back. Alexis's hands on it. Jake kissing her. Alexis kissing Jake. How the hell is this possible?

I pick up a silver bracelet and two pairs of silver and turquoise earrings that match. I hold them in my hand. Feel the smoothness of the silver; admire the blue of the turquoise.

"You serious about this?" Mrs. Elliot asks Alexis. I can tell she does not trust teenage girls. You got that right, lady.

"Yesss," Alexis says.

"I have a lot of real customers," Mrs. Elliot says. "Christmas shoppers." She points around with her head.

"My money is good," Alexis says loudly. *Bitch* is implied, but she holds back.

"You'd better not be wasting my time."

"Just open the case," Alexis says.

And as the saleslady puts the key in the lock, I very slowly and carefully, hiding what I'm doing with my body, drop the bracelet and both pairs of earrings into Alexis's open bag.

I feel better immediately. I go to the perfume counter and buy a bottle of Charlie for Grandma.

As I pay, I keep my eye on Alexis and the saleslady.

The bomb is ticking.

Alexis doesn't buy anything, of course. By the time we leave, Mrs. Elliot is seething. She lost at least five customers while Alexis was pretending to be serious. And Alexis has jewelry in her bag she hasn't paid for. I pray to the God of Revenge that she gets caught. I pray with the most impressive *kavanah* I have ever had.

"Let's go," Alexis says, still as if nothing is wrong. And I obediently follow her.

As if nothing is wrong.

We're making our way through men's shirts and suits, toward men's underwear and socks by the door, past men's cologne, when I hear Mrs. Elliot shriek, "That little thief!"

There it is.

Alexis keeps walking. So do I. But *I'm* not at all surprised when, the minute we walk out of Morrison's, a man in a suit, with an obvious earpiece, comes up next to us.

He grabs Alexis's arm and says, gruffly but quietly, "You will have to come with me."

"What, what?" Alexis says, pulling away from him. "I didn't do anything! I didn't. I swear. Not this time!"

A woman in a security guard's uniform comes up to me. My

heart is pounding wildly. I try to look shocked. Also upset. Shocked is hard. Upset, not hard at all. "What?" I manage to say.

The woman takes a look in my bag, sees my jeans with the receipt and Grandma's perfume with that receipt. I am shaking all over, but I guess that seems normal even if you are innocent, because Security Guard Lady says, "You can go. But we'll be watching you next time. We have your picture on surveillance now."

"OK," I say. And then, because I can't help it, "What about Alexis? What are you going to do to my"—uh—"friend?"

The woman raises one eyebrow at me, looks as if she's about to talk, but then doesn't say a thing. Instead she turns away and takes Alexis by the other arm.

The two of them lead her away, Alexis saying over and over, "I didn't take anything, I swear I didn't. I swear, I didn't take anything."

I turn my back and slowly walk down the street.

CHAPTER 22

TABLE FOR ONE

I do not run. Somehow I know not to run. Maybe they're watching. If I ran, they'd realize I am not the innocent girl I pretended to be.

Will I get away with it? Do I want to get away with it? Was it *just* revenge?

I hate her. Of course I want to get away with it.

I don't run. But I also don't look where I'm going and I bump into something—uh-oh, someone.

Oops—I've run right into a big lady, a Pennsylvania Dutchie in a puffy lavender jacket and a pink scarf, probably in from Lititz or Carlisle, to buy things she can't find in her small town. Why don't these people go to a real place, like Philly or New York?

Her big shopping bag starts to tip, and soon everything is going to fall out—but I grab it and I stop that forward motion; I stop the mess that is about to happen.

"I'm so sorry," I say. "Really, I didn't mean to—"

I'm sure she is going to yell at me for being careless, but instead she says, "It's no big deal."

I look up at her. "Really, I'm sorry."

"It's *really* OK. Hey, *you* OK, honey? You look like you seen a ghost!"

I have, lady, I have. I look into her nice, open face. Her arbitrary kindness makes me well up, and I want to confess all.

"I'm fine," I mumble, and walk on.

Within steps I have an ache in my heart, and I wonder if years from now I'll think I should have crawled into her plump lavender arms right then and there and let her make everything all right.

I can't believe I did that to Alexis.

No. I can't believe she did that to me.

What is happening to her right now? Are they calling the cops? Are they handcuffing her to a table? She deserves this. I swear she does.

But.

No.

No buts.

I could go back to Morrison's, make it right, but I don't. I keep walking.

I go to the Red Eagle Diner.

Shopping makes me hungry.

(So, apparently, does shoplifting.)

(Also, betraying my former best friend.)

(Also, finding out my former best friend betrayed me with my—boyfriend. Jake, how could you? Oh.)

I think of what *I* did last night and I start to lose my appetite. And yet . . . the smell of frying fat and salt lures me in.

• • •

I stand in line behind a mom and two little boys. After the hostess seats them, she comes back to me and asks, "How many?"

I say "two," because I am too embarrassed to say "one." I never eat alone. Especially after committing a heinous crime.

"You have a preference? We're not that crowded yet. Everyone's still shopping." Or being put in handcuffs.

"Could I—I mean we?—sit over there?" I gesture toward the window.

"Sure," she says, and leads me there. She puts me in a corner near the front, where I sit with my back to the restaurant, facing the window.

When she leaves, I have a fantasy. They let Alexis go, she comes to find me, and we laugh about this stupid joke I played on her. And the stupid joke she played on me.

Here's another fantasy: none of this really happened. Not what I did with Adam, what Jake did with Alexis, what I did to her. I didn't really shoplift and plant it in Alexis's bag. I only *think* I did it—like in a dream where you find yourself naked and you keep saying, I'm not really naked; I didn't just take my clothes off in the middle of the hall at school, did I? Oh, please, God, no! And then you *will* the bad dream to end and it does and you wake up and you are so relieved.

I pinch myself. I'm quite awake.

I see the waitress walking over, and I take out my phone and pretend to be on a call. She is about twenty, sweet-looking. No nose rings, no tattoos. The name badge on her pink waitress top tells me her name is Luanne.

"You waiting for someone?" she asks me.

I shake my head and put my phone down on the table.

She looks at me and says, "OK." She seems sad, or shocked. Not that many teenage girls eat alone.

"It's OK," I say. "My friend might show up." See? See? I want to say. I have a friend. OK, so it's an imaginary friend. I do have a real friend, but if she shows up, it will be with a cop.

"Do you want to wait just in case or order now?"

My waitress has more faith in my "friend" than I do.

"I'll order now." When Grandma and I used to come here, we got chopped salads with blue cheese dressing on the side. Alexis and I always get (got)—

"I'll have a grilled cheese and tomato, deluxe." Deluxe is the way to get fries without saying "with fries." So you can pretend you're surprised when the fries come. "On rye. And a Diet Coke."

"Thanks," I say to Luanne when she puts down my soda, almost instantaneously.

I squeeze some lemon in and drop it into the glass. Do people in restaurant kitchens wash the outside of lemons? If they don't, what if it has dirt on it? Or raw meat? Are you supposed to put the lemon into the soda like I did, or just squeeze it in? Why don't I know the answer to this?

God, what an idiot I am. I can't believe I did that.

Well, I can't believe she did that. With Jake. I can't believe he did that.

I can't believe I did everything I did.

"Here you go, sweetie." Luanne puts down my plate gently, in a very un-diner-like way. "Enjoy," she says.

I take a bite of my grilled cheese and—oh, God, I love the

salty, fatty flavor of it. I have heard of people who can't eat when they're upset. Not me, apparently. I enjoy every bite of my sandwich and all of my fries, which I have sprinkled with lots of salt. Every single bite.

When I finish, my plate is empty. There is not a speck of food on it. I have even eaten the mushy diner pickle.

I feel full, satisfied, not sick to my stomach as I probably should. Now I know what they mean by "comfort food." I should have bought the bigger size. Who am I kidding? At the rate I'm going I should have bought size 22.

I've lost everyone now. Everything.

Damn that Alexis.

As if I've summoned her, I look out the window and there she is, walking by. With her mother, who is holding her by the arm. I sat here for a reason, even if I didn't realize it.

Her mom is yelling, and Alexis is shaking her head, yelling back. I know exactly what Alexis is saying, and I know that her mother is not believing a word of it.

What I honestly do not know is how I feel about it.

CHAPTER 23

LOCKED OUT

A Monday morning to beat all Monday mornings.

I spent the rest of the day yesterday alternating between fury and terror. Every time the phone rang, I jumped out of my skin. It was never Alexis, or her mother, or Morrison's. Or Jake. As if.

It was either Grandma or about Grandma.

At five o'clock it was Mrs. Philips calling to say Grandma was wandering again. After that call, Mom fired the aide and Grandma spent the night at our house.

I did not give her the perfume. It seemed tainted. I was afraid it would burn through her skin. I put the bottle in one of my desk drawers.

After dinner, I helped Mom get Grandma in the den, put her to bed on the pull-out couch. When Mom bent down and kissed Grandma on the cheek, Grandma said, "You are such a good daughter."

And it hit me so hard, in my gut, sharp like horses' hooves, what a terrible, terrible, horrible thing I had done.

Even what Alexis did to me—if she really did it—cannot justify what I did to her. And to her *mother*.

After all they've been through. After all we've meant to each other. You don't just turn off a friendship like a faucet of scalding water.

The epiphany I had at that moment was that I have to make it right. Immediately. Alexis first. I will figure out the Jake stuff later.

I dress like crap because I feel like crap. I am crap. Baggy jeans, a black top that I don't look good in, and black sneaks and I'm done with it. I don't look in the mirror again. I go right downstairs to the kitchen.

Dad's pouring his coffee into a travel mug.

"Dad, can you drive me to school? I need to get there early."

Mom looks up from her laptop, gives me the once-over. I expect her to say something about the way I look, but she doesn't. "Why do you have to get there early?" she asks.

Before I can lie, Dad says, "I have to leave right away. You can come with me, but you'll get there really, really early."

"That's fine," I say, and fortunately, neither he nor Mom questions it.

School is practically deserted. I pass no one as I walk to my locker.

I get what I need for the first part of my day, and yeah, that takes about a second. Great. I have way too much time to kill.

Alexis's locker is right down the hall from mine. I could write her a note, slip it into her locker, instead of talking to her like I planned.

But what would I write? "I'm sorry I screwed you over. And by the way, screw you, too."

That would go over well. Besides, the thing is this: I am not that sorry. I am, but . . . I am more sorry about who I became when I did that than . . . for what it has done to her.

And that is the dirty, honest truth.

I think.

No it's not.

I don't know. I really don't. I am a flip-flopping mess.

What I hope is that we can figure it out together. Alexis and me. That we can actually talk about it all. That's what I really want. Which I couldn't accomplish with a note.

I fall asleep standing at her locker. The first bell startles me awake.

When I finally see her coming through the throngs, I can see she's had a hard night, too. Of course she has. Her face is pale, and even from far away I can see she has dark circles under her eyes. We have been friends for so long. I can't stop caring just like that. Maybe she can't either. Maybe we are even now and it will all be OK.

I am ready.

But she doesn't notice me. Or pretends she doesn't notice me. She goes to battle right away with her lock, which is temperamental. It usually takes her two or three times to get it open. For some reason I can do it better than she can. I think about offering, but she finally gets it. When she looks up to grab her books from the top shelf, I see her see me. I wait for her to acknowledge me, but why should she? It really is up to me.

I take a deep breath. "I want to make this right," I say.

"How the hell are you going to do that?" she says.

"I'll go into Morrison's, tell them I did it. Tell your mother. Tell everyone."

"They won't believe you, Rachel," she says angrily. "*I* don't even believe you, actually."

"Wha—?"

Alexis turns away and wipes her eyes. Is she crying?

"Lex—?"

"Look, you little shit," she says, whipping back around to me, her face bright red. "I've been caught at Morrison's twice before. After what you did, I'm never allowed back in there. Ever. Three strikes and I'm out, babe. They called the *police*. They fucking *fingerprinted* me, Rachel."

Oh, God.

"Why didn't you tell me?" I cry. "That you shoplifted and got caught?? I didn't know!"

Alexis shakes her head. Sighs. "How would that little talk have gone?" she snaps at me. "With sweet, innocent Raebee? Can you actually picture the two of us *having* that conversation?"

I hate her for saying this, but I know she's right. I would have been horrified.

"I want to make this right—I do. I mean, I'm still *furious* at you for what you said to Jake, what you *did* with him, but I want to make this right. OK? OK?" Pleading.

She looks at the floor. Says nothing.

"I really *am* sorry, Alexis."

She picks up her head and looks at me. This is the moment when she will yell at me, which I deserve, and then we will cry, hug, make up, and I will promise to go to Morrison's.

But no.

No.

"Fuck you, Rachel."

I look at her. Her eyes are dead.

"Oh come on, Alexis! We've been friends forever. Can't we talk about it? Fix this?"

The second bell rings. She slams her locker door, gives her lock a spin, and, when the bell stops, looks at me. "You are *so* not worth it," she says. And she walks away without giving me a glance.

CHAPTER 24
ALMOST AMISH

I wish I were Amish. I do. Or a Hasidic Jew. There's something about that kind of closed-off community that is appealing. All the rules are set for you, all the decisions made. Wouldn't that be nice?

The Amish do this thing that would be incredibly helpful right now. I'd convert for it in a heartbeat. It's called *rumspringa*, which means "running around." We learned about it on a field trip to Lancaster in eighth grade. They let their teenagers go off into the world and experiment. The kids drive cars, drink, fool around, do all these things Amish adults aren't allowed to. But the thing is, when the kids come back to the community—which most of them do—there are no questions asked and no punishments. They just take them back.

What I wouldn't give for *rumspringa*!

OK, everyone, I'm back! I was just kidding!

Lex, babe. *Alexis*, you hear that? I'm *back*. Jake, I'm here! It's me, the old Rachel!

But no. I don't have anything at all like *rumspringa*.

And I have no Jake. No Alexis. Having no Alexis at all, not even a distant Alexis unpredictably alternating with old familiar

Alexis, makes me realize just how alone I really am. Without her, without Jake, I'm just a sparrow in a flock of other sparrows. These other girls, the friendlets, are just sparrows to me.

Alexis was never just a sparrow.

I don't even have Adam. He has been ignoring me completely since the party. It's like I'm invisible. The Amish do that, too. They shun someone who's done something wrong. They don't yell at them or hurt them; they just ignore them. Maybe I've leapt into an alternate Amish universe.

When the Amish make a quilt, they put in a mistake intentionally, as if to say only God can make something that's perfect. Well, I sure have gone and made sure there are mistakes in my quilt. My quilt is all mistakes at the moment.

I keep trying to text Jake, but what would I write? I hope when I see him, I will brilliantly think of exactly the right thing to say, but he is not in study hall or in English class. I see the back of him in the hall once, so I know he's alive. But that's it.

By Thursday I'm desperate for human contact. So in history class I try talking to this girl Zoë. She's no Old Alexis, but she's intellectual and arty, veggie-crunchy. I like her.

Me: "That was a lot of reading last night."

Her: "I liked it. I like Howard Zinn."

Me: "Yeah, he's good."

Her: "I meditated after reading the homework, and it was, like, really a good meditation."

Me: Huh. Think of something to say. Think, think. Draw her out. "Yeah. Can you tell me some of your insights?"

Her: "Meditation is private, Rachel, I'm sorry."

Me: "Maybe you'll teach me sometime." God, am I reaching, reaching . . .

McKelvy says, "Anyone have any thoughts about last night's reading?"

Zoë's hand shoots up. "Zinn has great insight into the minority person's plight in this country." McKelvy nods his head happily, turns around, and writes on the board, "Whose country is this?" and underlines it three times.

Then he goes back and underlines *Whose* a fourth time.

What is it about some teachers and chalk?

Lunch is a real challenge. Where would I sit? So I've skipped it every day this week so far. Stayed in the library instead. Foodless. Those jeans look OK on me now.

But today is murder. I didn't have time for a real breakfast; it was raining, Mom had an early appointment, and she offered to drive me to school. I had only eaten a granola bar in the car ("Over a napkin, Raebee. Don't get my Prius dirty!"). And now the librarian, Mrs. Yankovitch, is heating up leftover pasta Bolognese. Her husband has been taking cooking lessons from an Italian chef. It smells way too delicious.

I head for the cafeteria. I'll sit at Zoë's table; she sits with yoga/tofu/vegan types. They'll probably ignore me, but in a peaceful way. The line is short, the service quick, and I have my tuna hoagie with the works within a minute. When I get to the veggie-crunchy table, Zoë is the only one there except for this couple, Chase and Autumn, who just started going out and can't take their eyes, or hands, off each other.

"Thank goodness you're here," Zoë whispers to me. "Everyone else is on a field trip with environmental science class."

"So you're left here with Goo-goo and Gaga," I whisper back, and she laughs.

It is so nice to hear someone laugh at one of my jokes.

In my newfound happiness I take a huge bite out of my hoagie. Too huge. I almost choke as Zoë stares at me, either out of disgust or concern. If I were her, I'd be thinking, Do I remember how to do the Heimlich maneuver?

I swallow finally and say, "I was famished."

She nods. "I was worried about you."

"Thanks," I say gratefully, and take another huge bite.

I don't know which would be worse—not finishing my hoagie or becoming the laughingstock of the cafeteria, because all of a sudden I realize everyone is looking at me.

But then I hear little sex noises, and I realize they're not looking at me. They're staring at Chase and Autumn, who are going at it so hot and heavy that they might be making a baby right here, very soon.

"Guys," Zoë hisses at them, "stop it! Too far!" Chase has his hand up her shirt. Autumn—oh, give me a break, she has her hand down his pants. The front of his pants. Yeah, I'd say they're going too far.

I totally know about losing control, that's for sure, but really—in front of the whole cafeteria? Can't they tell time has stopped still? There is not a sound—no clinking of dishes, nobody talking. Every single person in the whole place is completely silent, watching to see what will happen next.

All of a sudden a deep male voice booms right next to us.

"Hey, you two." It's McKelvy, who is lucky enough to have cafeteria duty at this historic moment. "Stop right now, or you'll have detention for the rest of your lives."

They don't stop.

"Separate detention. You will never see each other again." He's bellowing now, so everyone all over the cafeteria can hear him. Ohmygod. They still don't stop.

Finally, McKelvy whacks Chase on the side of the head, risking arrest, or at least being fired, but nobody, nobody, would turn him in. He is practicing an old-fashioned form of birth control.

Goo-goo and Gaga finally stop kissing. They pull apart, and the whole cafeteria starts clapping and whooping. Autumn looks around the room, gets it, and runs out, crying. Chase, on the other hand, pumps his fist into the air, and the crowd cheers. McKelvy grabs him by the shirt collar, pulls him to his feet, and says, "Detention for a week! Meet me in the principal's office after you've, uh, calmed down." I look at Chase's pants, and yeah, he'd better calm down.

Zoë and I laugh hysterically as soon as McKelvy leaves our table. So does everyone else in the cafeteria. Even Chase. For a few seconds I feel normal, and grateful to Chase and Autumn for being more screwed than I am.

The bell rings, and everyone starts to leave. I neaten up my tray and turn to say something to Zoë. But she's not at the table. She's vanished into the crowd.

CHAPTER 25

TIKKUN OLAM

I've almost made it through the week. Very few Jake sightings. He seems to have taken an invisibility pill himself. In a way I'm relieved. It hurts so much to think about him.

It's Friday, and McKelvy is supposed to go to Union with me today. He's never been to the reading lab. I'm glad he's coming. But maybe Randy won't even be there. No, Mrs. Glick would have called me if he wasn't going to be there. He'll be there. But what kind of shape will he be in? I'm nervous. I haven't been nervous since that first day.

Maybe McKelvy'll give me the inside scoop on what's happening with Chase and Autumn. My carrot as I trudge through the rest of the day.

Math class is fun. If *fun* is a synonym for *torture*.

I sit in the back, as usual. I know this is a bad idea. I should sit in the front row and pay close attention. Instead I let myself space out.

All of a sudden I hear, as if coming from a muted bullhorn, "Rachel, Rachel Greenberg, did you not hear me or are you ignoring me?"

Oh crap. I look up at the front of the room. He's got another one of those sequences on the board.

"I don't know," I say.

Mean Scary Math Teacher whips his face to the right and says, "Kenny?" to the math genius who sits next to me.

Kenny clears his throat, says, "I am trying to determine if there is a pattern to the integers, and what I see is that each one following is half the previous one plus two, but—oh, I get it!" He laughs delightedly. "Fantastic! It's thirty-seven, of course."

Of course.

Once again I think of Randy. I have *got* to help him.

When I get to McKelvy's room, he says he can't go. He has to deal with the Chase and Autumn situation, mostly a few "little repercussions" from whacking Chase on the head.

"I'm not going to get fired or anything," he reassures me when tears start to puddle in my eyes. "I have to explain why I hit him. I have to give them my justification, to prove it was legitimate. So, what was my justification?"

I laugh even though I want to cry. I guess I didn't know how much I was looking forward to his coming to Union with me. "The whole cafeteria will back up your justification. It's called birth control."

"Tell me about it," he says.

I want to give him a hug, but the last thing I want to do is get him in trouble for hugging a girl. I'm pretty sure he's gay, but just in case the Powers That Be don't know that, I'm not going to touch him.

"You'll go with me another time," I tell him, and I smile at him even as the tears spill out of my eyes.

"Are you OK?" he asks, but before I can say anything, his class phone rings.

"Uh-oh," he says as he picks it up. After he listens for a minute, he mouths, "Principal."

"I'm fine," I say. "Good luck." I give him a pat on the arm as I leave the room.

The minute I walk in, Randy runs to me with a huge pile of books and an even huger grin. My little boy.

"You're late!" he says.

"I am?" I look at Mrs. Glick. She shakes her head. I have made a point of not being late since that first day.

"Randy has been really eager for you to get here, so his teacher let him come down early."

"Wassup, dude?" I say to him.

He giggles. He always giggles when I call him dude. "I have a prize for you!"

"A prize?" I say. "Why do *I* get a prize?"

"I mean a surprise. Sit down!" he yells while he's jumping up and down.

Mrs. Glick says, "Randy, inside voice, please. I know you're excited, but . . ." at the same time I say, "Randy, dude, you're going to drop those books!"

"OK!" Randy whispers. The loudest whisper I have ever heard, and I erupt into giggles, too. We fall onto the car pillow, and he puts his head on my shoulder briefly. Maybe I'll never leave the reading lab.

"Which book do you want to start with?" I ask him. Randy pulls out a book. "This is a new one Mrs. Glick got for me," he says.

"*Go, Dog. Go!* by P. D. Eastman," I announce. I know this book very well. It has a dog in a car on the cover, but it's not about cars. "Randy, you sure you want me to read you this one?"

"No," he says.

"OK, so which one?"

"No—I mean, are you ready for my surprise?"

I nod.

Randy takes the book from me, opens it, and starts to read. "'Dog. Big dog. Little dog.'" He is not faltering at all. "'Big dogs and little dogs.'"

He looks up at me and smiles. I stare at him.

"Oh my gosh!" I say, tears filling my eyes. He's reading.

I should be totally and unselfishly happy, but I am not. I'm happy. But I also feel robbed.

"'Do you like my hat? I do not like it,'" Randy reads. With *expression*.

He finishes the book without making a mistake, not a single mistake. How did that happen?

"Randy, that was amazing! I am so proud of you!" I say, because I am, even though I feel let down. I wasn't there when *it* happened. I wasn't the one who taught him to read.

"When did you learn to read?" I ask him, willing myself not to cry.

"I don't know," he says, shrugging. "All of the sudden I saw the words—"

"His teacher called me—it was a few days ago." Mrs. Glick

is standing next to us. "She said Randy picked up a book and just started reading it. Sometimes, like I told you when you first started, it just clicks."

"It didn't just click," yells Randy. "I worked hard at it!" For the first time ever I see him angry.

"Of course you did, Randy. I know that!" I say.

"You sure did," Mrs. Glick says.

"I'm so very proud of you!" I say. Thunderstruck is more like it. But I am happy for him. I AM. He got it. Himself. This is the best thing that could have happened. "SO PROUD!" I yell in a Randy voice.

"Thank you, Rachel," he says, and gives me a big hug. "I love you."

I want to tell him, No, you don't love me, you love yourself. But instead I say, "I love you, too, Randy." And we spend the rest of the period in a reading-and-love-fest.

I stay after class, and Mrs. Glick and I beam at each other for a few minutes. I am totally over feeling cheated. I am beside myself with happiness for Randy. It's so great he did it himself.

"It's huge for him," Mrs. Glick says.

"But the rest of his life is in the toilet," Mrs. Washington says. "His grandma's got end-stage cancer."

"How bad?" I ask, stupidly.

"She might only have weeks left," Mrs. Glick says.

"I heard days," says Mrs. Washington.

"What does this mean for Randy? Where will he go?"

Mrs. Glick shakes her head. "We don't know."

• • •

I walk the whole way home. It gives me a lot of time to think.

There are no cars in the driveway. I'm disappointed. I wanted to tell Mom about Randy. But at least nobody's kissing someone she's not supposed to kiss in the driveway. I push that thought away fast.

I see Mom's taken chicken out of the freezer to defrost. I open the fridge and can tell what she's planning to make for Shabbat dinner: roast chicken with potatoes and carrots, a salad on the side. It's one of her usual dinners. I've helped many times.

I turn on the radio. It's set to NPR. I don't change it. I want someone else's thoughts in my head for a change.

I wash the chicken and pat it dry. It's almost defrosted. I brush the roasting pan with oil, very lightly, though I'm not sure if I have to. I can't remember if Mom does that or not.

I put the chicken in and season it with salt, pepper, garlic powder. What else? I shake on some oregano and basil. I have no idea if that's what Mom does, but . . .

OK. Next. Should I scrub or peel the potatoes? I bet Jake could tell me. They're those nice red ones, so I scrub them. I toss them in a little olive oil and garlic salt and then grind some black pepper on them, put them around the chicken. I peel the carrots, cut them up a bit, and throw them into the pan, too. Oops, I forgot to preheat the oven. I set it to 425° F, and while it's heating up I wash the lettuce and spin it dry. It's my least favorite job, so I change the station to music. A mostly oldies station. I wash and spin to the Beatles. I like them. Even if Alexis doesn't. "Alexis who?" I say out loud.

In some ways it's a relief to be done with her. Or at least to know where I stand.

When the oven beeps, I put in the roasting pan and go back to the salad.

Rufus Wainwright is singing "Hallelujah." I *love* him.

What about dessert? Do I have time to make something? If we have apples, I could make apple crisp. Or is that being too ambitious? I think of Randy's face beaming with pride. I think of his grandmother. Apple crisp it is.

I find apples, flour, brown sugar, butter, and get to work. I'll put it in the oven when the chicken is finished. It'll be ready by the time we're done eating dinner.

"Yesterday, all my troubles . . ." No way. I switch the station to indie rock.

I lose myself in the cooking and the music. As I'm finishing assembling the crisp, Mom comes in, muttering to herself about how late it is.

"Oh my God! What smells so good? Did I clone myself?"

"Hi," I say, turning down the music.

She looks at the apple crisp, peeks in the oven, and throws her arms around me.

"Rachel, you are a lifesaver!" she says into my back. I turn around so we're in a real hug.

"I got stuck at the Laudenslagers' house, and I didn't know what I was going to do about dinner. Grandma's coming, and I'm taking her to temple, so we really need to eat by six-thirty. Thank you! Oh, thank you!"

Is she crying? I hold on to her as long as possible.

Dad comes in the door with Grandma and a challah from our favorite bakery just as the timer beeps.

"Perfect timing!" I say.

"You cooked?" asks Dad, and I nod.

Dinner is delicious—everyone says so. Mom and Dad seem OK with each other, and even Grandma seems more or less normal.

When I bring in the apple crisp, they are knocked over.

And—Glory be to God!—no one pressures me into going to temple. Mom asks once, halfheartedly, if I want to go, but when I say I'm too tired, she lets it go. Dad and I do the dishes, and then he goes downstairs and I go into the den and watch TV.

When Mom comes in, she bends over and kisses me.

"Thank you so much for making dinner, Rachel. I love you." I can't get out the words "I love you, too" without crying.

I have been such a bad girl.

I squeeze her really tight for the second time today. And then I spend the rest of the weekend plotting.

CHAPTER 26

FLOODING

I've gone over and over in my mind the order in which I should do things. The *keva* of my atonement.

Should I go to Morrison's first? Alexis's mother? Should I talk to my own mother? Should I confront the rabbi? I mean, he started the slide into the hell that is now my life. Maybe if I confront him, chase away those demons, I will be back to where I was. Who I was. In my heart I know I will never be back to where I was, but.

But.

But I always end up at the same place. And it surprises me. Jake. I miss Jake. I miss who I am when I'm with Jake. I want him. I need to have him on my side. Then I will have the strength to do everything I need to do. Is this totally retro? I don't care. I need my boyfriend.

On Monday I corner Jake by his locker first thing in the morning.

"Walk home with me," I say to him.

"Why should I?" he asks with a harshness to his voice I find in no way sexy.

"*Tzedakah*. Charity," I say.

"*Tzedakah* actually means fairness, justice," he growls. I swear, he growls.

"Please, Jake? Will you give me a chance? Please?"

He looks at me, and then he nods.

"OK, Rachel," he says, and my heart lifts. I don't know how our talk will go, but this moment, right now, gives me hope. And a line from an old Joan Baez song Mom loves plays in my head. "Speaking strictly for me, we both could have died then and there." Really. It would be fine with me.

But we don't die, as romantic as that would have been. Instead the bell rings, and we go off to have our very earthbound high school days.

After school, I see him leaning against a tree. His back is to me, and although somebody else could mistake him for one of the other four hundred boys in the high school, every cell in my body knows it's Jake.

"Hey," I say when I reach him. It's all I can manage.

"What's up?" he says. I shake my head. No one ever expects an answer to that question, and I can't speak right now anyhow.

We start down the street. It's a mile and a half to my house, and to Jake's, but in about a mile he has to turn left and I have to turn right. I worry about that moment for the first couple of blocks. But that's all that's worrying me, because for some reason Jake is acting like everything is OK between us. After all this time. I don't get it, but I go with it gratefully.

At first we talk about school and classes and other stuff. I catch him up about Randy, and he's so happy. We both have McKelvy, different periods, so we compare notes on the last test we had (we both got As, though his A was a little higher than mine, damn it) and the papers we're writing. I'm writing about Katrina, he's writing about election fraud. It's so easy talking with him; I don't have to hide my smarts or my ignorance. I ask him a lot of questions, he asks me some, too, and it's just *so good*.

And then out of nowhere, as I'm pontificating, "Do you know more than fifty levees and floodwalls failed? Fifty! And because of that . . . ," he pulls me toward him. He kisses me hard, harder than I really want to be kissed. I almost pull away, but I don't. Because I want to keep kissing him.

The kisses get gentler and start to feel good. Really good. We drop our messenger bags by our feet so we can hold on to each other, and soon we move behind a big tree and kiss and kiss, and I feel him against me, and dreams come back to me quite vividly, dreams I hadn't let myself remember, as I reach my hand up into his jacket and up inside his T-shirt and I feel his back, strong and hard, and I am vibrating, vibrating, and, oh, that's my phone, which I ignore, ignore that and everything else as he reaches his hand up the back of my shirt and then down into the back of my jeans, and I feel him touching me and my phone starts vibrating again and I'm vibrating all over and then a car honks, and someone yells out of the window, "Get a room," and we pull away from each other, laughing, embarrassed.

Jake touches my cheek, my hair, pushing it away from my face. "I've missed that!" he says, his face hot, flushed, his voice hoarse. "I've missed *you*."

"Me too." Understatement of the millennium.

We stare at each other, eye to eye, really looking. It is almost unbearable.

"I am so sorry," I say. "About what I did with Adam. I am *so*, *so* sorry."

"OK," he says softly.

We both step back a little, pick up our bags, and start walking again.

"So, are you OK about it?" I ask. "Really?"

"No. Not completely. But I'm ready to talk."

He stops, looks at me.

"So," I say, "why are you ready to talk to me now—I mean, why did you say you'd meet me today?"

"I've missed you. And . . ."

"And?"

"I guess I don't believe you really did go all the way with him that night, at that stupid party, in that basement? Did you, Rachel?"

"No, of course not."

"Good. But . . . I mean, even if you didn't—though you didn't—you still fooled around with him. You cheated on me. You betrayed me!"

He turns away from me, says, "I shouldn't have kissed you just now. I shouldn't have. I *am* still mad."

There's a piece of me that wants to accuse him of what he did, but I push that away. This is *my* fault. I started it. I take a deep breath, walk around him so we are face to face.

I look him in the eyes. His beautiful eyes.

"Jake, I was really, really stupid that night. I completely lost control."

I wish I could blame pot, but that was a lie. A lie I told myself. I could blame the rabbi, Alexis, Adam. I could. Yet I know it's nobody's fault but my own.

"I—I was just—stupid. And I never, ever wanted to do anything to hurt you. I swear."

Jake stops, looks at me. There are tears in his eyes. "I want to forgive you. I do."

My heart is beating wildly, I feel sick to my stomach, but instead of pleading I say, "But?"

"But how do I know you're not going to cheat on me again? How do I?"

How do I know you aren't going to cheat on *me* again? I want to ask aloud, but I don't. Instead I say, "I won't, Jake. I won't."

He looks at me hard. "If you really care for me, and . . ."

"I do, Jake. I do care for you. So much."

"Let's walk for a bit," he says, and he takes my hand.

His hand feels so good, so strong. I want to just enjoy this moment, but I can't let myself. I have to tell him about Morrison's.

"Jake—I—there's something else."

"Wait, Rachel, I have to tell *you* something. I am scared to tell you, to ruin it, but . . ."

I don't say anything.

"I fooled around with Alexis."

I nod.

"She really came on to me. It was weird, and I didn't want to, but I was hurt and . . ."

"Yeah, I know. She told me. I didn't believe it, but . . ."

He doesn't say anything for a while, keeps walking.

"Did you really sleep with her?" I ask him.

"WHAT?" he yells. "NO! No way. We made out. She wanted more, but I said no. Rachel, I'm not an idiot!"

"I didn't think so. But she said—"

"I'm sure she did. Shit, I was embarrassed enough by what I did do with her. That's a big part of why I haven't been, you know, coming back to you. . . . I was too pissed off at myself, even though I was angry with you. It all felt so complicated."

I nod. "Yeah," I say. When did this happen, that life got so hard, so frigging complicated?

He stops, turns toward me, takes my face in his hands. "I only wanted you that night, Rachel. Only thought of *you*," he says quietly, and my heart leaps. Maybe it shouldn't. Maybe I should question this, but I look back into his eyes, and I know he's telling me the truth.

I wonder if Alexis knew—knows—he was feeling that way that night? She probably hates me. Well, I *know* she hates me. Which brings me back to my awful reality.

"There's still something else, Jake," I say, and before he can say anything, I barrel on. "I did something really horrible after that."

"You fooled around with someone else?" he says, looking upset.

"No, no, no."

Jake stops walking, turns to me, but, thankfully, doesn't let go of my hand.

"How bad could it be, then?"

I could go back. Just make a joke. "Bad," I say. "I think maybe worse."

"Oh, Rachel, you know deep down I can't believe you'd do anything really bad," he says, and kisses me lightly on the cheek. I turn to kiss him, not lightly, on the mouth, to change the subject, but I stop myself. I pull back a little to look at him, but I can't. Too nervous. Instead I look beyond him and see two little girls on tricycles, a mom watching them.

"Let's sit down," Jake says, gesturing to the curb. We walk a little farther up the street, where there aren't any cars parked, sit. He puts his arm around me and gives me a little squeeze. Oh, that feels nice.

"Tell me," he says. But he is *so* not prepared. I can tell by the indulgent way he says "tell me." This is not good.

But maybe what he's saying is, Nothing you could do would be that bad. So I start.

"You know how Alexis was caught shoplifting? At Morrison's? Did you know about that?"

"Yeah, I heard. But she said that you did it and planted the jewelry on her. How ridiculous is that?"

"You didn't believe it?"

"How could I? You would never do that, Rachel!"

Um.

"Yeah, well . . ." I take a breath. I smell Jake. That smell of his that I love—lemon and chlorine and sweat, the Jakeness of him.

I take another breath. "It's true. I did that. I took stuff, and I put it in her bag. I hoped she would get in trouble. I *wanted* her to get in trouble."

Jake takes his arm away. Turns to me. "Are you kidding?"

I shake my head.

"Why? Why would you do that?"

Because I really messed up. Because I *am* really messed up. I look at the ground.

Jake doesn't say anything.

Finally, I speak. "Because I was mad at her. For lying to you about what I did with Adam. For seducing you—she told me right before I did that. And just—she's been really mean to me for months, and . . . And then, that day, she was really awful to me, and I didn't really plan it, Jake. OK, I sort of did, not, like, ahead of time, just at the moment, and I just . . . I just . . . I *had* to get back at her. And I did."

I am blabbering. I decide to stop.

Jake moves away from me. Breathes deeply as if, I don't know, as if he needs fresh air after sitting so close to me.

"You told Morrison's, right? Told them it was you who did it?"

I shake my head, and even I can't believe it as I say, "No. I haven't. Not yet." Lame, lame, lame.

Jake jumps up from the curb and walks away a few steps and then comes back to me, hands on his hips. He's angry. I can tell he's trying to control himself, which makes me feel worse.

"I was going to, I was. I *am* going to. I told Alexis I was sorry, almost right away, and I told her I would go to Morrison's, but she said don't, and then . . ."

Why didn't I go anyway?

Jake looks down at me.

"I have other stuff going on, and . . ." Uh. Of course I should have gone to Morrison's right away. But she was so awful, and Mom and Dad are fighting so much, and Grandma, and the rabbi, and the rabbi and *Mom*, and still I don't know, no excuse, none, and oh damn, my phone is vibrating again.

I am a worthless piece of shit. I put my head in my hands.

"Listen, Rachel, I don't like Alexis very much, especially since that night. But still, you shouldn't have done that, and you should have told the store by now. How could you not? I don't get it. *It's just not like you.*"

"I know," I say, picking up my head and looking at his knees, not at his face. "I know."

"So you'll go into the store, right?"

I don't answer.

"Rachel . . ."

"I don't know!" I yell.

"You have to tell them. You have to!" He is not yelling, but he wants to be, I can tell.

I know he's right. Of course he's right. But what if I do and it sends my parents' marriage over the divorce edge? What if it breaks my grandmother's heart?

What if the person you respect the most disappoints you beyond belief? What if that person is you?

"I am not perfect!" I shout. "Nobody is perfect!" I jump up, stand facing him now. "Nobody is perfect!" I shout again, tears streaming down my face. I bet those little girls have stopped in their trike tracks and are staring at me. I can't look.

"This is worse than not perfect. This is wrong!" Jake is shouting now.

"Why are you being so hard on me?"

Jake shakes his head.

I hate him! How can he be so holier-than-thou? What makes him think he's so great? So above it all? Like he hasn't made any mistakes?

"Look, Rachel, it's like what the rabbi says."

The rabbi? The effing rabbi? "What does the *sainted rabbi* say?" I yell.

"You have to have *kavanah*, right? What was your *intention* in that moment?"

I don't say anything. How can I? I had *kavanah*. It was evil *kavanah*.

"And the rabbi also says . . ."

Oh, God help me. Not more with the rabbi.

". . . if you do something wrong, you have to ask for forgiveness and atone, right? I mean, we learned that, what, back in nursery school? You have to make things right, for God's sake. That's what Rabbi Cohn would say, and he's right."

"Rabbi Cohn? Fuck Rabbi Cohn! Jake! I heard him screwing someone on the *bima*. He's a terrible person!"

It just came out, and I can't help myself, I keep going. "And I think he's having an affair with my mother, Jake. He's a bad, bad man!"

"What are you *talking* about?"

"It's true."

"I don't believe you."

"Believe me," I say. "Believe me."

I want to walk away. But I can't. I know it's the only way through this for me. So I stay right there and I tell him. It all comes rushing out. About that night, everything, every detail. My mother and His Holiness in the driveway, my searching for clues. I tell Jake all of it.

He looks shell-shocked.

"Do you believe me?" I ask him. I so badly need him to believe me. I've waited so long to tell someone, someone who would believe me, would care as much as I do, and it's Jake. It's always been Jake.

He shakes his head no, then nods. "I can't believe it, but I don't think you're making it up, either."

"I'm not," I say.

"Wow," he says, and we're both quiet for a few minutes.

I hear screams from the little girls on the tricycles. I look at them—they are racing each other; happy screams.

"Jake—"

"Look, Rachel," he says, "I know that the world can be a shitty place. It *is* a shitty place. People are born wrong, and die, and people do stupid things, terrible, immoral things."

"Tell me about it."

"He really—you really heard that? Rabbi Cohn? And your mom really was kissing him, too?"

"Yes," I barely manage.

"I still can't believe it, but . . ." He sighs, looks at me with what I think is kindness. Could be pity. "But I do. I do believe you."

"Thank you, Jake. I—"

"But this thing with Alexis, it's not who *you* are, Rachel. It's not. That much I know. And I think you know it, too, don't you?"

I nod.

"Rabbi Cohn . . . Wow . . . Some things make sense to me now . . . Some things I heard my parents saying . . . Oh boy . . ." He shakes his head sadly.

He looks a wreck. His hair is a mess, his face is red and pale at the same time, his eyes are wet, he's so very intense and his eyes are so beautiful and I think of him cooking for me, and I think of the feel of my head against his back, and I think of that little boy in the photos, and I want to feel him next to me again, and I blurt out, without thinking, without planning, but even so, I swear, with more *kavanah* than I've ever had about anything, "Look, Jake, I think—I *am* in love with you, and if you like me, or"—can I really be saying this?—"even love me a little, then please take me for me, the real me, not the me you thought I was, all good and pure and perfect, but the me who is real and makes mistakes and is still good at heart, I swear, and maybe I will do the right thing about this, and I hope I will, but I need you to help me, please help me, and please don't leave me."

So here I am, out on a damn limb, and I'm way far out, and the limb is too skinny and it is shaking.

I wait for Jake to answer, my head down, my eyes closed; I pray for his answer, and I hear his intake of breath before he speaks—he is about to speak—and then here is a car pulling up next to us, I can hear it, and Jake says, "Rachel," in a weird voice.

I look up at the car. It's my dad. He looks horribly upset.

"Grandma's in the hospital," Dad says. My phone. Vibrating this whole time. Oh no.

"How did you find me?"

"I've been driving around for almost an hour."

"I'm so sorry. What happened?"

"Heart attack," says Dad. "Massive."

"Oh God!" I cry out. The tears that were already there flow faster, harder. "I don't know what to do," I sob.

"Please get in the car," says Dad gently. "We're going to go to the hospital. Mom is waiting for us."

"I'll help you," Jake says. He opens the car door, helps me into the front seat. He buckles my seat belt for me and closes the door. He opens the back door and puts my messenger bag back there.

Dad pulls away very quickly, so quickly, practically burning rubber, but even so, when I look out the window for Jake—God I will need him now even more—to see his face, see whether he's with me or not, all I see is his (beautiful) back walking away. Walking away from me.

CHAPTER 27

GOING BACKWARD

The next week and a half passes in a blur. "Hospital time," Dad calls it. Grandma is in such terrible shape. She's hooked up to all kinds of machines in the Cardiac Intensive Care Unit; she's in what they call a light coma. A light coma? What would a heavy coma look like? They don't know if she's going to make it, or if she does, what her life will be like. What *she* will be like.

The ICU rules are strict. Only two people can visit her for fifteen minutes at a time. Mom is in there as much as possible. I take turns with Dad and Uncle Joe. But mostly it's Mom and me, because both Dad and Uncle Joe find it too sad. Grandma looks unbearably tiny and fragile in that hospital bed. And she's got all these tubes and wires stuck in her.

Sometimes, when it's quiet and no doctors are around, the nurses let Mom and me stand by her bed and talk to her for as long as we want. The nurses say she can hear us. (The doctors say not. We choose to believe the nurses.) Mom and I tell her stories, and we say "I love you" over and over again. I bring her up to date about Randy in the reading lab, how the last time I was there he read to me. I remind her about how she used to take me shopping, and how she taught me to make a Spanish omelet, and even about the time I got her on a bike down the shore and she wobbled and we laughed and then rode five miles together. When I talk to her like this and hold her hand, I don't mind the way she looks. In my mind's eye she is the Grandma I remember from my childhood. Not the Grandma from this past year.

Sometimes I ride to the hospital on my bike, but it's a long way from our house. I can't wait to get my license. I'm getting better at driving every time Dad gives me a lesson. Though I haven't left the driveway, since I'm not sixteen yet.

It's been pretty good between Mom and Dad since this happened—which seems like a lifetime ago. I haven't been in school since. Dad called and told them the situation, and they said I could stay out. Nothing much gets done around Thanksgiving anyway. Jake and I have texted a little bit, but nothing much. I told him what was going on; he said he was sorry about it. He was going to relatives out of town for a couple of days.

We had awful turkey in the hospital cafeteria on Thanksgiving. Just the three of us, since Uncle Joe had gone home to his family. It was sad, but for the first time in a long time we felt like a unit, Dad making dumb jokes, Mom and me laughing at them. It's been that way since, and they haven't made me go back to school.

But today Mr. Wonderful waved his magic wand again.

The three of us were in the waiting room because they were doing some procedure on Grandma. We were alone in there, thankfully. Not like yesterday when that dad and his kids came in sobbing because the mom had been in a horrible car accident. That poor family.

Dad was doing a crossword puzzle. Mom was pretending to read a magazine, but I could tell she wasn't. My hint? It was upside down. The two of them seemed a little off but not horrible. Mom closed her eyes, and I think she sort of fell asleep. So I sat next to Dad and did the puzzle with him.

"What's a five-letter word for *storm*?" he asked me.

"Storm?" I said, and he laughed.

Mom jumped a little, opened her eyes, gave Dad a look, and then closed her eyes again.

I wanted to kick myself. I made it worse somehow. But I was in the minor leagues compared to what happened next.

The rabbi walked in.

The rabbi walked into the waiting room.

The rabbi walked into the waiting room, and he nodded at me and my father. Then he sat down next to Mom and tapped her on the shoulder and said, "Evelyn."

She looked up at him and fell into his arms, crying.

"Oh, Rabbi," she cried. "Oh, Rabbi."

Oh, for God's sake, I thought.

The rabbi put his arms around my mother and pulled her to him. He held her, stroked her hair, her back. He rocked her a little. I couldn't stop watching, like it was a car crash.

I heard my dad mutter something under his breath, and then he slammed the newspaper down on the chair next to him, got up, and walked out of the room.

The rabbi kept stroking my mother's hair.

I stayed for a few minutes, but she kept crying and he kept holding her and stroking her and murmuring to her.

I got up and walked out, too. I should have followed my dad, I guess. But I had no idea what I'd say. None.

So, since it was Friday, I thought, what the heck, I'll go down to Union. I found out from the hospital information desk where to get the bus, and took it. Texted Dad that I was going.

I got to the school at the right time, but when I walked into the reading lab, Mrs. Glick shook her head and came over to me.

"He's gone. I tried calling you at school. They told me you weren't there and so I called your house, but no one answered."

"My grandma is in the ICU."

"I'm so sorry."

"What do you mean, Randy's gone?" Did she mean he died? I held on to the desk next to me. Was I going to lose everyone I cared about?

"He didn't show up at all this week, and no one answered at home. Yesterday, someone finally picked up and said that Randy was leaving town, wouldn't be back at school."

"So where is he, where did he go, why?"

"I don't know, Rachel. I'm still trying to find out. But my best guess is that his grandmother died and some other relative took him."

"Can we find out?"

She shook her head, frowned. "The best I could do was confirm with social services that he isn't in the system. So he's not a foster child anywhere."

"But how do we know he's OK?" I said, my voice cracking. "I don't think I can take not knowing."

Mrs. Glick clicked her tongue.

"Do you know where he lived?" I asked.

"What are you going to do?"

"I'm going to go see what I can find out."

Mrs. Glick wrote an address down on a piece of paper. I put it in my pocket.

"I shouldn't really have done that," she said. "But I trust you to be careful."

I went to the office. "Do you know where this is?" I asked the secretary who always calls me honey.

"Not far from here. Down this street two blocks and make a left."

So here I am, right where I wandered that first day. But today I don't feel at all uncomfortable like I did then. So what, I'm rich and I'm white and I'm Jewish. I'm not that rich. And I can't help it that I'm white. Jewish, well, I guess I'm still Jewish.

It takes me only a few minutes to get to the address. It's a run-down apartment house. There are some moms with toddlers outside.

I go up to one of them.

"Do you know a little boy named Randy? Randy Gamez?"

"No," she says.

"I know Randy," says another woman, an older lady. "His grandma died. She was raising him."

"I know," I say. "Do you know where he's living now?"

"What are you, a social worker?"

"I'm in high school," I say. I'm flattered that she thinks I'm that old. "I'll be sixteen in a month. I worked with him at his elementary school. Helped him with reading. I want to know if he's OK."

She shrugs her shoulders. "I guess. He went to Jersey to live with his mama's cousin. The guy's been here before. Then I saw him the day of the funeral. Packed little Randy up right after and left."

"What did he look like, the cousin?"

"I don't know. Young, wearing jeans and a baseball cap, you know, backward. I didn't really notice because they were just getting into the car."

"What kind of car?" I ask, impatient now. I have a feeling I'll know if Randy is going to be OK by the kind of car the cousin drives.

"Funny you should ask that. It was an old car, like one from thirty, forty years ago, a model I remember. But this one, it was all spruced up, shiny. Nice looking. Randy seemed excited, was asking the cousin all kinds of questions about it. Blabbin' away like his grandma didn't just die."

"Was the cousin answering?"

She looks at me like I'm crazy, but then she says, "Yeah, he was."

"Was he nice about it?"

Finally she smiles. "The cousin? Yeah, he was really into it. They got into the car chatting up a stream."

"Thank you," I say to the lady. "Thank you!"

And thank you, I say to God.

I am going to let myself feel good about this.

What else can I do?

CHAPTER 28

GOING BACKWARD II

It's close to midnight, and I'm woken up by them yelling at each other. Then doors slamming, feet stomping. Damn, I thought they were doing better. That rabbi. I swear. He ruins everything.

I hear an engine start. Which car is it? Who's leaving this time? It's usually Dad. What am I saying? It's always Dad. I crawl quietly across my bedroom and look out the window. Mom's car is still in the driveway. Yup. Dad. Again. Where does he go? He goes somewhere but then ends up here, sleeping on the couch.

I have to know where he goes. If I hurry . . . if I take a bit of a chance . . . I've done it enough times with him. "If you can back out of the driveway," Dad has said, "you'll be able to drive, no problem. Reverse is the hardest."

I am only in my flip-flops and sweats, but I don't care.

Her purse is on the table by the door; her key right on top. I'm going to get in so much trouble. Visions of police cars, sirens blaring, dance in front of my eyes, fill my ears. But I don't care. My poor Dad.

What has my dear, sweet, singing, curtain-opening, joke-cracking Daddy done to deserve this?

I get into the driver's seat in Mom's car and immediately realize two things: I have never backed the car down the driveway in the dark, and I have never backed a car down the driveway without Dad right next to me.

But if I don't hurry, I won't find him.

I push the power button as I've seen Mom do and put my foot on the brake. And then I realize one more thing: I've never backed Mom's car down the driveway. I've never actually driven this car. She wouldn't let me.

Tough.

I put it in reverse. It starts *beep beep beep*ing, shattering the quiet of the night. I can't see out the back, and then I remember the screen—this car has a video screen for seeing out the back. Do I have to press a button to turn it on? I fumble around, and as I push the button, I realize I've turned it off, not on, and I push it again, but it doesn't turn on, and meanwhile the car is going backward, and so I forget about the screen. I also forget about the slight curve in the driveway and the bump where the tree root has pushed it up at the end, and I forget that Dad always warns me about all of that and his Japanese maple that's right there at the side at the end and—

Thwack. Thud.

Crunch.

Mom's beloved Prius just hit Dad's beloved Japanese maple. I have never heard anything so awful.

Not since "Oh, Rabbi."

But this sound is worse. Because this one I made.

CHAPTER 28A

GOING BACKWARD III

I sit stunned for a minute. Terrified.

Shit, shit, shit.

I have to get out of here, get out of this. If I run into the house, put back the key, and pretend I'm asleep, maybe they'll think it rolled on its own. Mom forgot to put on the emergency brake or do something. . . . I don't know with this car, it's practically alive, maybe . . .

But first I have to see how bad the damage is. Maybe it sounded a lot worse than it is. I pray to the God I'm not sure exists. . . .

"Please let it be nothing. Please, please, please."

I open the door—it opens fine!—and walk around the front of the car to go around to the back left side, where it hit. I walk around the car this way to put off seeing the damage. Giving me a few seconds of hope. I pray some more. I bargain.

"I will go to Morrison's if you let this be nothing, just a little scratch," I say to God, who must certainly exist. "Please let it be a teeny-tiny scratch. I swear, I will make everything right. I will. I promise." What if God has only one favor for me? It should be that Grandma not die, not this. But I don't really believe—

"Please, please, please," I whisper to the dark night air. Hey, maybe I'm dreaming! I can definitely lucid dream my way out of this. I jump into the air, like you're supposed to do to figure out if it's a dream or real. If it's a dream, when you jump, you fly.

I do not fly. I land, hard, on a driveway rock, in my flip-flops.

"Ow! #%*@###!" I make up a curse because nothing else is strong enough.

I hurt so much I don't delay the inevitable any longer. I look.

Oh, God. You dirty rat.

Oh, Rachel. You stupid jerk.

My mother's beloved Prius has a huge dent, plus a smashed rear light and a broken hatchback window. There is glass on the ground.

A light goes on inside our house.

What about the Japanese maple? Dad planted it the week after I was born, in celebration. We have all these pictures . . . every year on my birthday.

I force myself to look, and it is still standing, but that is all I can tell.

They are going to kill me.

I need a plan. I have to get out of here. Where will I go? I have nowhere to go.

I hear a car door slam. "Evie! Evie! Oh God!"

I turn around, and there's my father running toward me. His car is parked way down the street, down the hill from our house. That's where he goes?

When he gets close enough to see it's me, he cries out,

"Rachel, oh no, Rachel! Honey, are you OK?" and then he runs faster and he's there and he's giving me a hug. Not what I expected. And his face is wet. He's crying. Is he crying because he was worried, or was he sitting in his car crying?

Or both?

"Are you OK?" he asks me.

"Are you?"

And we both shake our heads.

"Dad—" and "Rachel—" we say at the same time, but then, "What the hell is going on?" Mom. "What was that noise—is the car . . . ? Rachel? Dan? What the HELL is going on?"

And before either of us can say anything, she sees the car inserted into the tree and she lets out a bloodcurdling scream.

"Shhhh!" my father says. "The neighbors are going to call the police!"

"Good!" she says, glaring at me. "Was this you? What were you thinking?"

Dad starts to talk, but I speak over him. "I was looking for Dad. I was *worried* about him."

She turns and hurls at Dad, "It's all your fault!"

"What?"

"You taught her to back out of the driveway!"

Dad laughs. He laughs? "Well, obviously not very well." He's laughing hysterically now. I think. Maybe he's crying.

"Oh!" she says. "I'm going to kill you. Both of you."

"Are you thinking you have no part in this?" he says to her.

Go, Dad.

"What are you talking about? I was inside!" Mom yells.

"He was crying in the car!" I shout. "Right down the hill. You drove him out and he was crying in the car."

Dad does not deny it. No one says anything for at least a minute. A minute that seems like a year.

Does my saying it make it worse? I want to take it back. Not name it. But I also want to yell about what else happened in this driveway. But then Mom moves toward me, grabs my arm so it hurts, and says softly and slowly but distinctly, "Rachel . . . go . . . back . . . inside . . . and . . . go . . . to . . . your . . . room. We will . . . talk . . . about . . . the . . . consequences . . . in . . . the . . . morning."

"But . . . ?" I look at Dad. He's no help. His head is down.

"Go. Now," she says.

"Go, Raebee," Dad says, and so I walk backward up the driveway, very slowly, figuring they can't kill each other as long as I'm watching.

CHAPTER 29

LIGHTNING

Dad and I are sitting in the waiting room, waiting for the moment of truth. Not in the hospital but in the Crunch-A-Bunch Auto Repair Shop. I am terrified to hear how much it's going to cost to fix Mom's car. It's all on me.

My life is going to suck, but I deserve it. After a long lecture and many tears (mostly, but not all, mine), they decided that I would do whatever chores they asked me to do at home now, and also babysit, and then get a job this summer, to pay off the bill. They don't want to go to the insurance company because it'll raise their rates, especially since I'm about to come of driving age. Oh, and I can't get my license until I'm seventeen. I begged and pleaded and cried, but I got nowhere. And I'll get nowhere that I can't get to on my bike. But that's OK, because I have no friends. And I'll be working so hard to pay off the bill, I won't have anywhere else to go but work.

My fingers itch to text someone—Jake, Alexis, one of the girls, even Adam, but no. This is where I am now. Alone. Alone in a car repair shop with my dad. And since I'm about to get bad news anyway, and Dad's miserable as all get-out, I figure what the hell, let's spew all the shit at once.

"Dad—I . . . Can I . . ." He's reading *Men's Health* and doesn't look up. Must be that cover story I saw, "Your Prostate and You."

I sure do hate to interrupt. Must be captivating. "Dad!"

"Rachel?" He gives me a half smile.

"It's not about this—this car thing—but I have to tell you something."

He puts down the magazine, takes off his reading glasses.

My heart lurches. I love him, my Daddy, and I'm probably about to ruin his life—if I go that far, which I decide right now I won't. I don't have to. I'll only tell him . . .

"What is it, Raebee?"

I don't look at him. I look over his shoulder to a poster on the wall. There's a big-boobed blonde in a bikini standing next to a red car with yellow lightning bolts painted on it. GIVE YOUR CAR A BOLT AND ELECTRIFY YOUR LIFE, the headline says. Oh please.

"It's awful, icky," I say.

"About you?" Dad asks. His voice sounds so scared. I was going to tell him about Morrison's. I was, I was. But I can't.

"No, not exactly. I mean, I— Can I just tell you?"

He nods.

"Dad, back in October I— Oh, Dad, I heard something. I don't know how to say it."

"Do the Band-Aid thing, Rachel, just rip it off quickly—"

"Still hurts when you do it that way, you know. I've been meaning to tell you that for years."

"I know, honey. It's not that it hurts less, it hurts for less time."

"Well, OK. But it's going to be hard. To say and, I think, to hear."

Dad swallows. I see his Adam's apple bob up and down. "I may already know," he tells me.

"I doubt it," I tell him, but I wonder what he's thinking he knows.

"Go on."

"So, one night I went early to confirmation class because you and Mom were fighting." Oh, why did I have to say that? I'm a chicken, a blamer, making it his fault, their fault, which I now realize I've always thought it was, without really knowing it. If they hadn't been fighting, I wouldn't have left early, I wouldn't have gone into the sanctuary, I wouldn't have heard. . . .

"We've been doing that too much lately," Dad says. "Fighting in front of you. I'm sorry about that."

I have to keep going. "So, I got there early and I sat in the sanctuary and—" I shake my head, no, don't. I can't tell him. Dad touches my arm, pats me. I forge ahead.

"I heard the rabbi." Band-Aid. "I heard the rabbi having sex. Right there in the sanctuary, Dad. And it—the woman wasn't Mrs. Cohn. It wasn't his wife, Daddy."

I look at my father. He's looking at me expectantly, fearfully. I wait for him to say something, anything.

And then he does. "Was it Mom?"

CHAPTER 29A

LIGHTNING II

"Mom? How could it have been Mom?" I say. "She was home with you, fighting. That's what I said. Why would you say it was Mom?"

"I don't know. I know. I'm just . . . I'm so confused, so scared," Dad says, and he is crying. Right there in the stupid auto repair shop. I had been planning to tell him about Mom and the rabbi and the kiss in the driveway, but no way, not now. And then Bob, the mechanic, comes out, wiping his hands on his coveralls.

"Dad," I say, nudging him. "DAD!"

My father looks up, doesn't even wipe away his tears.

"I'm afraid it's going to be a lot," Bob says, looking at me, not at my father.

I nod. "Tell me," I say.

"OK," Bob says. "To repair all the damage, replace the light, and paint it—we'll have to paint the whole back end so that it looks good and even—" He stops.

"Band-Aid," I say. "Just rip it off."

Bob laughs, ruefully. "Two thousand, maybe more, give or take."

I wait for my father to argue, bargain, cajole, or tell me I don't have to pay it all. He says nothing.

Bob goes over to the counter and writes on a sheet of paper. I clear my throat to speak, but then I don't. What can I say?

Bob comes back, hands my father the paper.

"Two thousand?" my father says, looking down at the numbers. He stares at the paper for a while, but I can tell he's not really looking at the particulars. He picks up his head and looks at me. "OK?" he says to me.

What am I going to say? It's like when you pay for something in the store and the electronic screen says, "The amount is $26.09, is that OK?" and you want to say to the screen, Well no, not really, I'd rather pay a lot less. How about $12.95?

"OK," I say. "OK."

CHAPTER 30

FLYING SOLO

The more I pedal, the better I feel. And the worse, which is the point. It is cold out, but I am in fleece, and I am sweating. It's the middle of the day, so no one is outside.

I am feverish. Fluey. Or maybe it's just emotional. Who knows? I am not going to the hospital, in case I'm contagious.

When Mom left to go sit with Grandma, she made me promise to stay home. Why would she think I would leave?

But she was right.

I'm going to go confront the rabbi. Finally. I am going to confront the rabbi. I'm sure this is what I have to do. He's what started my whole slippery, careening downslide, and I think the only way to commence to begin to start to try to climb back up is to go back and do what I should have done when I first heard what I heard. I can't do anything to save my grandmother. I can't bring myself to upset my parents more and confess at Morrison's right now . . . so.

Or—and this thought occurs to me as I near the temple—I could make it all worse. Oh God.

Oh God, I am so mixed-up. Oh God, I wish you were still here.

I don't think God disappeared when I heard what I heard or because of it. I think He (or She) was gradually disappearing already, fading from my life like the people in the old photographs in Grandma's living room.

God used to live on my bedroom ceiling. (This was after I figured out that Rabbi Cohn wasn't the same as God. As if.) I used to have conversations with Him most nights as I fell asleep. God was also in temple on Friday nights, but that was really a different God, a public God, the God I shared with everyone else. The God on my bedroom ceiling was my own personal God. And I depended on Him.

Then, when I was in sixth or seventh grade, before my bat mitzvah, I realized that I was thinking of God as She. Not that He had had some kind of transgender issue, a transsexual sex-change operation. Just—God was definitely a woman. And then, I don't know, after the bat mitzvah, after a while, I stopped talking to Her. To God. I realized She couldn't be on my bedroom ceiling only at night, and I knew She wasn't there during the day. So then I thought maybe God was inside me or floating around, but I only really thought about God when I needed something, like an A on a test, or for someone not to die, or at Yom Kippur when I had to tell God all I did wrong that year. But if I am honest with myself, now I think of God the same way I think about the tooth fairy.

I seek out the hills. I struggle up the steep ones and then turn around to fly down them. I am not suicidal. I am wearing a helmet.

But I would like to end up really sick in the hospital, down the hall from my grandmother, so that everyone would worry about me and stop being such idiots. Mom and Dad would stand by my bedside holding hands. The rabbi would realize his mistakes, and Jake would forgive me. He would love me. And maybe Alexis would, too. If I almost die, everybody will love me. I will make everything all right.

I remember when I got pneumonia in third grade and was in the hospital for two weeks, missed six weeks of school. I don't remember being scared, but I did think I might not ever get better. Mom told me later that I almost died.

She sat with me all night, holding a cool washcloth on my head. There were hushed conversations by my bed between her and Dad, her and the doctors. I remember when I got hungry for the first time in weeks and craved McDonald's french fries, Mom ran out and got them for me at ten o'clock at night.

But mostly what I remember is how close Mom and I were. When your nose itches and you can't scratch it because you're holding something, you ask someone to scratch it for you, but it never works. They can never scratch it in the right place, the right way. Well, one day Mom scratched an itch for me.

When I got home from the hospital and started feeling better, all I really wanted to do was to fly that great kite I had gotten for Hanukkah. But I was still too sick. I could barely move. One day the weather was perfect: a late March afternoon, clear sky, windy but not too much wind, just the right amount. Mom wrapped me up in a blanket and put me on the screened-in porch at the back of our house. She got out the kite—a huge bird, black and red and yellow, about six feet long.

I sat there, shivering underneath the green and gold afghan

Grandma had made, watching Mom run up and down the backyard. She yelled and cheered for the kite, trying over and over again to get it to fly. Our backyard has trees on the edges, so she had to be really careful not to get it caught.

"It's not going to go up," I said to myself. But she heard me.

"Oh yes it will, Raebee. I got you well enough to come home, I'm going to get this kite to fly."

Finally it caught the wind, and oh did that bird soar! It stayed up there for a long time, dancing in the wind, and I slowly got out of my chair to stand at the edge of the porch. Watching Mom and the kite, I felt like I was out there flying it myself. I *felt* the wind tug at it, I *felt* the kite find the breeze. Mom turned to me often to look at my face, which was one huge grin. After a while, the kite started to shake. Because Mom was shaking.

Crying. Sobbing. I could hear her. I wanted to go out, but I was too tired. So I sat back down in my chair and watched and waited.

Eventually, the wind changed and the kite floated down. Mom came in, her face tear-streaked.

"You flew it for me," I said to her.

"Yes I did," she said.

I pedal and pedal, working up as much of a sweat as I can.

When you're little, your mom can make the world all right, most of the time. But when you're older . . . and when she's part of the problem . . . well, shit.

I would do almost anything to feel my mom's hand on my forehead, feel her arms around me, and think that she is pure and good and all-powerful.

But you can't go back, can you?

I tell myself it's OK.

I tell myself it's better to be older and to know what's what. I tell myself it doesn't feel the same to watch somebody else fly a kite. You have to fly it for yourself.

CHAPTER 31

EVERYTHING I NEED TO KNOW I LEARNED IN . . .

It's not that I chicken out, but when I get to the temple, I have an epiphany: it's not about the rabbi. Not anymore. It is way beyond that.

I have pictured the scene so many times: I go into his office. I tell him what I heard. He denies it at first, but I give him details, salient details. He looks chagrined, apologetic. Or angry, defiant. He cries. He laughs, evilly. Threatens me. No, I know he wouldn't do that. But what could he do that would make it better?

What I come down to is this: there's nothing he can say that will undo what he did, and more so, what I have done. I am furious at him, I am, but I don't blame him anymore, not really.

He started the ball rolling, but I'm the one who made the touchdowns. I think I just mixed sports metaphors, but I don't care.

I get off my bike and sit down on the curb across from the temple. Almost immediately, as if to prove my decision correct, the rabbi comes out of the building and walks to his car. How could my mother, the Prius lover, have kissed a man with an SUV?

He stops, turns around, looks at the temple as if he's left something there, but then opens the car door, gets in, and drives away.

When I'm sure he's gone and not coming back, I walk up the steps, slowly, dragging my bike with me. I prop Sir Walter inside by the front door. I plan to go sit in the sanctuary, to Get Over It, but that's not where my feet take me.

They take me to the kindergarten room. The room where I first fell in love with the rabbi. The block corner where Jake and I used to play. The brightly colored rug, finger paintings on the wall, the smell of Play-Doh. It all comes back to me.

Tiny little-person chairs, the blond wood cracked and stained, do headstands until they are rescued and set right.

I take one down, try to sit in it. I do not fit, of course. Not anymore.

He sat on that big oak desk and played his guitar for us. He told us about right and wrong, about atonement, about the golden rule.

I text my mother.

`I'm going to sleep. I'll call you when I wake up.`

And I do sleep, right there on the rug in the kindergarten room.

I wake up to noises—oh no, not again—but these are knocks, not groans. I look up. Someone is standing outside, on the playground. He is knocking on the glass. It is not someone I want to see.

Adam motions to me to come outside. I shake my head, and he makes a sad face and crosses his heart. It's a promise of some kind. OK.

I rouse myself, walk out through the glass door.

"What are you doing here?" I ask him.

"I could ask you the same question."

He sits down on a swing and lights a cigarette. I sit on the swing next to him.

"Why do you smoke?" I ask him. "You're going to die before you're twenty."

"I should be so lucky."

"Very funny. Why do you have such a death wish anyway?"

"Why were you in the kindergarten room?"

I look at him. Shrug. "Why are *you* here?"

"Well, first I was getting reamed out by my father. Now I'm planning how to burn down the temple."

"Very funny again."

"I really am. Don't you think it's a great idea?" he asks me, taking a big drag. "Make it seem like my Dear Old Dad did it."

"Huh," I say articulately, and I kick the cedar shavings under my feet.

"Wow," he says. "Rachel, who has an answer for everything, has no answer for this."

"If you think I have an answer for everything, you have no idea."

He looks at me. "Why do you hate him so much all of a sudden?" Adam asks me.

"Who says I do?"

"Well, it's pretty clear. I don't think he's the only one you hate, but . . ."

What is *that* supposed to mean? I push myself and start to swing hard and high. Adam does the same thing, and soon the swing set starts to shake, and it feels like it's going to fall over.

"Shit," Adam says. "I guess this is not made for big kids." And he laughs, swinging even harder and higher.

I slow down and, as soon as I can, stop myself by touching my feet to the ground. "You better stop, too," I tell Adam, getting off.

He doesn't.

I stand back, near the slide, and watch him swing for a few more minutes. With me off, the thing is not going to fall over. But he's still being reckless, swinging high, holding on with only one hand so he can keep smoking.

"Adam, come on," I shout. "You're going to get hurt."

"You care?"

"Yes I care," I say.

Adam slows himself down and then jumps off the swing and comes over to me.

Before I can stop him, he kisses me, starts to put his hand on my butt.

"Dude!" I say, and pull away. "Shit, Adam! Are you so one-track?" I shake my head and laugh a little.

"But you said you cared."

"I do care," I say.

"You do?"

"Yes, I do." And I realize it's true. "You're my friend. But *just* my friend, Adam. Not my boyfriend, not my fool-around buddy, but my friend. Can you handle it?"

"Aw . . ." Adam kicks at the dirt. "You sure? Just friends?"

I nod.

He walks back over to the swings and sits down on one. He doesn't swing. Motions me over. I sit down next to him.

"OK?"

"If that's what you want," he says to me.

"That's what I want," I say. "What about you? Do you want to be friends?"

"Yeah. I'd like you to be my friend," he says. "I'd like to be *your* friend. I really would."

"Good," I say.

"And I'm really sorry about—you know, everything."

"Me too."

"I'll give you your shirt back."

"My shirt?"

"From the party."

"Oh, thanks," I say, and we put our arms around each other for a second, swing to swing.

"Hey, did you really do that to Alexis? At Morrison's?"

"Yeah," I say.

"Dude!" Shakes his head. "Man."

"I know, pretty stupid. I'm going to have to fix it."

"Yeah," he says, shrugs. "I guess."

"So why do you hate your father so much?" I ask him after a few minutes of silence.

"Let me count the reasons," he says.

I don't say anything.

"Everyone thinks he's such a great guy," he says.

"I don't."

"You used to."

I nod. "Not anymore."

"You tell me why you don't think he's a great guy anymore, and then I'll tell you why I have hated him since I was nine."

"Why should I go first? What if I say something horrible about your father and then you tell him and . . ."

"That's not going to happen, Rachel."

"Please," I say. "You first."

Adam takes out another cigarette, lights it, inhales long and hard. I'm going to make him quit.

"He makes a fool out of my mother," Adam says, and blows smoke toward the building.

I take the cigarette out of his hand and stub it out on the pole of the swing set. He doesn't light another one.

"He cheats on her. All the time. These stupid women go to him for marriage counseling and he sleeps with them."

Mom? Oh, Mom.

"He preaches about being good and honest, the fucking hypocrite."

Adam walks over to the slide and sits at the bottom of it. I want to ask him if he knows if my mother is—but he has his head in his hands and, oh, Adam is crying.

"Adam." I walk over and put my arm around him. I hold him and let him cry. He slows down, picks up his head, goes to light a cigarette, but I take the pack from him. He doesn't protest.

"Give me the lighter, too," I say. He squeezes it in his hand.

"Please."

Shakes his head. "Might come in handy."

"Adam, you were kidding about setting fire to the temple, weren't you?"

"Listen, Rachel, there was this rabbi, in New Jersey, and he had his wife killed, and he almost got away with it, so I could—"

"Don't even say it, Adam."

"No, I wouldn't have Abba killed, but I would flame this place, make it look like he did it so he'd get put in jail and . . ."

"Oh, Adam, please!"

"Yeah, see, I've thought about it. I have a plan."

"Adam, that other rabbi, the one in New Jersey, isn't he in jail? He *didn't* get away with it!"

"That's just the point. My father wouldn't either."

"Yeah, and neither would you, Adam."

"No, I would. I'm smart enough."

I look at him.

"I AM smart. I'm not book smart like you, but I'm really smart."

"You're also out of your fucking mind."

He looks at me. Starts to laugh, and tears roll down his cheeks again.

"You can't do anything like that, Adam. Promise me you won't. That you won't do anything stupid? Promise me?"

"Why? Why should I promise?"

"Don't let him ruin your life any more than he has, Adam. You have the power. You do."

"I do?"

"Yes. Promise?"

He shrugs.

"Give me the lighter."

I stick my palm out. He gives it to me.

"I can always get another one, you know."

"I know. But don't. Now say it."

"I promise."

"Say it."

"I have the power."

CHAPTER 32

GOING DOWN(TOWN)

I walk into Morrison's through one of the revolving doors, and like a scene in a comedy I find myself outside again.

Breathe, Rachel, breathe.

I turn around and go back in through a regular door.

"Can I give you a spray?" a very made-up woman asks me. Does she think that's pretty?

And why would I want to put on men's perfume? We are in the men's department after all. "Is it for men?"

"No. It's for you. It's called Truth," she says. Of course it is.

"Sure," I tell her, "go on ahead."

"You like it?" she asks, and hands me a coupon.

I smile vaguely and walk away.

How, exactly, am I going to do this? Is there an office where you go to confess a crime? I could act suspicious near the jewelry counter and hope I get picked up. I remember Grandpa once told me that the easiest thing to shoplift was a canoe. No one would believe you hadn't paid for it as you walked out of the store holding it high above your head. Why would he have told me that? He was a lawyer, honest to a fault. Could not tell a lie. There must be a lesson for me in that story, but damn if I know what it is.

On Task, Rachel, On Task. I'm in the middle of men's underwear. A clerk is giving me the hairy eyeball. What would that look like, exactly, an eyeball with hair coming out of it?

Oh, for goodness' sake. I am totally losing it. And my nerve.

I grab myself by the scruff of the neck and do the only thing I can think of. I go to the jewelry counter and ask Mrs. Elliot's advice.

"You shoplifted something how long ago and you want to confess now?"

"Yup. Or I could put a canoe over my head."

She looks at me like I'm a creature from another planet—certainly not Planet Teenage Earth. "Huh?" she says.

"Yes. Sorry. I shoplifted some stuff and someone else got blamed for it. I need to make it right."

"Do you have the things you shoplifted?" she asks.

"No," I say.

"Then how, what—"

"Look, I planted them on a girl I was with right here, at your counter," I say, and it sounds so horrible I can barely get out the rest. "And—she—not I—she was caught. And I was let go."

Mrs. Elliot looks at me. "So why now?" she asks, not unreasonably, I guess.

"If not now, when?"

She shakes her head.

"Look, I can't stand it anymore. It's eating away at me, OK? And I am here. Now." And there I go, tears streaming down my face.

"OK, don't move." Mrs. Elliot picks up her phone and punches in a few numbers. Here we go. I called Alexis this morning, twice, and she didn't pick up. Finally left her a message, telling her what I was about to do.

"Sam, we've got a girl here who says she wants to confess a shoplift." She looks at me, her eyes searching mine. "No. I don't think she's a flight risk. Yup. At my counter. OK."

"What should I do?" I ask when she hangs up.

"Wait here; Mr. Lawrence will be right down."

OK. This is so stupid. I should leave. What was I thinking?

"You're not going to run away, are you?"

I shake my head. "Tired of that," I say, and all of a sudden I am so tired. I wish I could put my head on the counter, take a nap. I start to do that—put my head on the counter—I really do, but then there is a man standing next to me, and a woman, too. The man is dressed in a suit, the woman in blue jeans and a polo shirt, carrying a purse, dressed to look like a shopper, I guess. But I can see she has a little earpiece in, and so does he.

"OK," he says. "What have we here?"

The woman has taken my upper arm and is holding it gently but firmly enough that I know if I started to bolt, I would not have a chance.

The three of us start to walk away, and I look at Mrs. Elliot. "Thank you," I say. And "I'm sorry."

She nods briskly and starts rearranging things on the counter. Or is she looking to make sure I didn't swipe anything?

The store detectives, or whoever they are, are the same two as before, the ones who grabbed Alexis, I'm pretty sure. They walk me to the escalator, and we go up one flight, walk through women's clothing, past the restrooms, and down a hall I've never noticed before. We go through some double doors, and then we are in a regular work kind of hallway with offices on both sides. We walk into one of the offices. It has a beat-up wooden table with chairs around it. We all sit down.

"So?" the woman says. I'm sitting on one side of the table, the two of them are facing me. He's got a yellow legal pad in front of him, a pencil in his hand.

Kavanah.

"My name is Rachel Greenberg," I say. I wait for them to tell me their names, but they don't. His is Sam. Sam Lawrence, I guess. Hers I have no idea. But they just stare at me.

OK. "A few weeks ago I was in here with my friend Alexis." I hear myself say the word *friend* and want to correct it, but I don't.

"Huh," he says, and he asks for her last name.

"Bloom," I tell him.

He writes it down, and nods. He remembers who she is.

"So," I continue, "you"—I look at him, Sam—"caught her shoplifting and, I think, took her to the police or called the police and they had her fingerprinted and stuff? And now she can't ever come in here again and—"

He nods. "I definitely know who she is, believe me. We had *caught* her twice before, though I know there were times when she lifted stuff but we didn't catch her. Anyways, we have a three strikes and you're out policy."

"Yeah, well," I say, "she didn't do it that time. I did."

Sam looks at me, shakes his head. "It's not going to work, Miss Greenberg."

"What? What's not going to work?"

"You can't take the fall for her. I'm not letting her back into this store. I'm not undoing what was done just because you come in, what, three weeks, a month later and say you did it? Fuhgetaboutit."

"No, I—" I hadn't thought of this possibility. Shit, shit, shittity shit. I get up, walk around the room. I can tell they think I'm going to bolt, so I walk over to the window that faces the street and look out. I can see the diner from here. What was that waitress's name? Damn. I can't get it. Leslie? Laurie? Joanne?

"I know what you're thinking," I say, turning around. I go and sit back down. "But I'm telling the TRUTH, I swear. I took a bracelet and two pairs of earrings. From Mrs. Elliot's counter."

Sam gets up and walks out of the room. Woman and I sit there without saying anything until finally I ask, "What's your name?"

She shakes her head.

After about five minutes of Very Awkward Silence, Sam walks back in. I was about to ask if I could go to the bathroom, but too late for that now. I have to pee. Bad.

"Well, Rachel, that *is* what we caught her with, but how do I know she didn't tell you to come in here and say this? That she didn't prime you with all the details? There isn't even a record of her being with another girl. Why should we believe you?"

"Look at the tapes. You'll see me there, I swear!"

"We tape over those things," Sam says, "once a case is resolved."

"But it's not resolved!"

What am I going to do? I put my head in my hands and try to think. There's got to be something. Finally I get it.

I pick up my head. "Call her mother," I say. "Not her, but her mother. See if she'll come in. Alexis probably told her mother that I did it, and she didn't believe her."

They look at each other.

"Call my mother, too," I say. "Or both my parents. I'll tell all of you at once. No way would I do that if I weren't telling the truth, right? My grandmother is in the hospital right now. She's in the ICU and she's probably going to die." The words catch in my throat. I can't believe I said that out loud. "Trust me, this is not a good time—it's an awful time—but I can't stand it anymore." My mother is going to kill me.

Sam and no-name woman stare at me.

"Please?" I say. "Please."

Sam grunts. "OK. Give us the phone numbers."

CHAPTER 33

BURSTING

They leave the room to make the calls. I am left alone. If I don't get to the bathroom soon, I'm going to burst.

If I go look for a bathroom, one of two things will happen: either they will tackle me, thinking I'm running away, or I *will* run away. So I stay in the room, pacing until I can't stand it anymore, sure that the pee is going to start coming out—I don't think that would be a good move on my part—and so I sit down, with my legs crossed tight. Praying someone walks in soon.

My prayers finally are answered, the door opening with a bang.

"Rachel, WHAT is going on? I was at the hospital with your GRANDmother, for God's sake, and then I get this call, and what am I to think?"

"Hi, Mom. Listen, I have to go to the bathroom. I am bursting."

Mom looks at me like I'm nuts, shakes her head, exasperated. "Rachel, as if I don't have enough to deal with right now! First my car, and now this. What were you thinking?"

"Mom, Mom, I know, but could you help me find a place to pee, please?"

Mom looks at me, and I guess her mother instincts kick in, because she leaves the room and a zillion bladder-bursting minutes later she comes back with a key with a wooden L dangling from it.

"Come on," she says.

We walk down the hall, away from the door to the main part of the store, away from my easy exit, and she opens a small one-person bathroom for me.

I pull down my pants and experience heavenly relief. I swear to God, I can't remember what I drank, but I pee a bathtub.

"Yeah, I'm here," I hear Mom say outside the door. "No, I don't think you have to come down. OK, come. Good. Thank you. Please, could you do me a favor and check the home messages, make sure the hospital hasn't called there? I know but . . . Thanks, honey. No, no idea. I don't know if it's a plea for attention or what. Yeah, OK. OK. Uh-huh."

In spite of what I'm in the middle of, of what I'm about to go through, I'm hanging on every word, and I almost smile when I hear the *honey*.

My phone vibrates; I have a text. It's from Jake. Is he psychic? I haven't heard from him in so long.

I click to open it, my heart racing.

`Rachel, how is your grandmother? I'm thinking of you. Jake.`

I text him back.

`I'm at Morrison's, Jake. But Grandma very sick. Thank you.`

He texts me right back.

`Good for you.`

And then,

`I am so sorry about your grandma.`

Wow. Maybe everything will be OK between us. Wouldn't that be nice? More than nice.

I walk out of the bathroom thinking about Jake, and possibilities. I must have a smile on my face, because my mother stares daggers at me.

As we get closer to the room, I hear Alexis's mother's voice. It's going to happen. I breathe a sigh of relief. Finally.

But when I see Alexis's mom, I start to cry. I can't help it. I used to love Ginny, being at their house. The tears start rolling down my cheeks, and I can't stop them. I don't know how I'm going to get any words out. Mom takes me by the elbow and sits me down, kind of hard. Sam sits down next to Ginny, across the table from me and Mom. Woman sits at the head of the table. Shouldn't they put a tape recorder in the middle of the table?

It is perfectly quiet in the room. Then Sam clears his throat.

"Well?" he says.

I force myself to stop crying.

I look at Ginny. "You know when you got a call from Morrison's and had to come pick Alexis up because she shoplifted?"

"Which time?" she says angrily.

"The last time."

"How could I forget? It was one of my worst moments as a mother. Thanks, I'm gathering, to you?"

I nod. "What did Alexis tell you back then? Do you remember?"

"Of course I remember! She said she didn't do it. But I didn't believe her!"

"Did she say I did it?" Of course she did.

"No. She had some lame excuse like somehow that stuff must've gotten in her bag but she had no idea how."

Are you kidding me? Had she not figured it out? Or was she protecting me? Could she have been? What about—what about after I told her?

"Did she ever tell you that I did it? That I planted that stuff on her?"

Alexis's mom shakes her head.

"Are you serious?" I didn't know I could feel worse about this than I already did. "Why wouldn't she tell you? She hates me. Why wouldn't she tell you the truth?"

Ginny starts to cry. "Because she knew I wouldn't believe her. She knew I thought you were such a good girl and she was a lost cause. . . ."

I put my head in my hands. I wonder if I will ever have a child.

Sacrifice your son, your only son, God said to Abraham.

"Hee-nay-nee," *said Abraham. "Here I am."*

Here I am.

And when God calls out to Adam in the Garden of Eden (not to Eve, of course), but when God does that, God *must* know where Adam is. God knows everything, right? But it's up to Adam to show himself.

I look up. Everyone is staring at me.

"I should have done this much sooner. Right away. I didn't, and I'm really sorry about that. But I am here now. I'm really, really sorry. I hope you will forgive me, but I won't blame you if you don't."

"Why don't you tell us what happened?" Sam says.

And so I do. I leave out the part about Alexis calling me a fat slut. I leave out the part about her being nasty to Mrs. Elliot. I leave out the fact that Alexis fooled around with my boyfriend, that I had been traumatized by the rabbi having sex on the *bima*, that I was in a state because my parents' marriage was in the toilet. I don't say any of that. All I say is "Well, Alexis and I were having kind of a fight."

I tell them with *kavanah* exactly what I did, how I did it, and the order in which I did it. The *keva* of my shoplifting experience. As I recite the details of the day, I realize I never gave Grandma the perfume I bought her. And now it's probably too late. I grab on to the edge of the table so I don't lose it, and I finish the story with my slow walk to the diner. I don't mention the lavender lady. I don't mention my grilled cheese and fries. Luanne! That was her name. Luanne.

I've been staring at my hands on the table. When I am finished, I look up. But I can't look at anyone. I look at the door.

No one speaks. For the longest time.

Finally Sam says, "Miss Greenberg, I just have to ask, if this is all true—and I'm still not sure it is—why are you coming forth now?"

How can I explain it without sounding ditzy or preachy or phony? Or nuts?

Just then my father comes in.

"Anything from the hospital?" Mom asks, her voice frantic.

"No," says my father. "Everything's the same." He looks sad. Boy do I feel like shit. But seeing my dad, and remembering how he cried in the auto-repair shop, and thinking about that stupid rabbi, I feel strong.

"Back when I was a kid," I say, "I could do stuff and not take responsibility. You know? When you're a kid, they say, 'She's just a kid.' But I'm almost sixteen now, and—" I was supposed to take responsibility from the time I had my bat mitzvah on. That's what the rabbi said the day of my service. I remember it clearly. I shake my head. The rabbi.

"Anyway. Look. There's so much sadness in the world, people who do bad things, and I don't want to be one of them. I don't want to add to the sadness. That's all. And I can't keep hating myself."

Again no one says anything.

"Can you please expunge Alexis's record, or whatever it is you do? It's not fair. I did it. She didn't! Make it right, please!"

"OK," says Sam, "I will take it under consideration. I believe you are telling the truth." His voice is soft, almost kind. I can't stop myself. I start to cry again.

I want my mother to hold me to her, to hug me. I expect her to. But she doesn't.

I wait for her to put her arm around me or for Dad to come pat my back. But she doesn't. He doesn't. They don't.

And so I put my head down on the table and cry by myself.

CHAPTER 34

OUT OF BREATH

They have not said a word to me or to each other since we left the store.

I don't know what I expected. I thought maybe they'd yell at me, or maybe even, God forbid, praise me for doing the right thing. But they are utterly and completely silent. I hate silence.

Well, *I'm* proud of myself. I am.

When we get home, my parents continue the silent treatment. They go straight into their bedroom and slam the door.

I hide in the corner of the living room so I can hear what they say. The wall is right up against their bedroom wall.

"It's our fault," I hear my mother say. I can hear her crying.

"No it's not," says Dad. And more soft murmurs from him that sound like he's comforting her.

"We've been fighting so much," she says.

"True," he says. "But we've also been under a lot of stress."

"It's my fault," says Mom. "Dan, I really think she saw the rabbi kiss me in the driveway."

I wait for my dad to shout, yell, walk out, slam the door. But he says, "Well even if she did, what does that have to do with shoplifting and planting it on Alexis? I don't think you can take the blame for this one, Evie."

He knows? He knew? Wow. When did she tell him?

Mom says something I don't hear, and then Dad: "She did something really wrong, and it's nobody's fault but her own."

"I thought I knew her, I really did," says my mother.

"I know," says my father. "Me too."

I want to die.

"You did know me," I whisper. "You still do."

There is nothing more from their room. I hope this means they're hugging each other, which is what I would like more than anything in the world. A hug.

But I guess I'm not going to get it. Not now. Not anytime soon.

I pour myself a glass of water in the kitchen. Well, it's over. There's nothing more for me to do. It's done.

And then the phone rings.

I hear Dad pick up in their bedroom. I pick up in the kitchen.

Who is it? The police? Alexis's mom?

"Another massive attack . . . lack of oxygen . . . severe brain damage . . . slowed respiration . . . matter of hours . . ."

Dad hangs up and so do I.

They walk into the kitchen and see me standing there.

Mom looks shell-shocked. Dad has his arm around her, holding her up.

"You heard?" he says. "Please call Uncle Joe. We're going to the hospital."

"I'm coming with you."

They don't say no.

I get into the backseat of Dad's car and call my uncle. I reach him in Kansas City; he's traveling for work. He won't make it here in time. He starts to cry, and I pass the phone to Mom. She talks to him for a minute and then hands me back the phone.

"Thank you," she says.

"Thank you for letting me come," I say, and she starts sobbing.

We get to the hospital and park, and as we're walking up to the front door, Mom grabs me in a big hug. She doesn't say anything, but she hugs me tight. Walking in, Dad puts his arm around me.

"Thank you," I whisper.

When we get up to the ICU, the nurse in charge tells us they've moved Grandma to a private room. Mom and Dad talk to a doctor. Mom signs papers.

Then, while we wait, they disconnect everything—all the tubes, monitors, oxygen, everything. There is nothing left but for her to die.

Mom sits on one side of her bed and holds her hand. I sit on the other and do the same. Mom talks to her, tells her how much she loves her. She doesn't cry while she talks; I don't know how she does that. I won't be able to. So I just stroke Grandma's arm for a while. Her skin is still so soft, and she is warm.

I am going to miss her so much.

The thing is, she doesn't look like herself at all, not even her recent self. She is so tiny, so pale, so old, so lifeless. I had been losing her for a long time, ever since Grandpa died. This lady here, this was not my grandma.

But she was my grandma, and I need to tell her that.

"Can I have a minute alone with her?" I ask my parents.

"I don't know, Rachel," says Dad, looking worried.

"It's fine," says Mom. "She can handle it." And she and Dad walk out of the room, their arms around each other.

I know I will remember the next few moments for the rest of my life. I tell my grandmother how much I love her. I say all of my favorite things about her, my most wonderful memories. And then I promise, "I will keep you alive, Grandma. I will tell my children about you."

We stay through the night. I sleep a little, but Dad and Mom don't. And then, just as the sun comes up, as the room gets lighter and the morning noises of the hospital start, Grandma breathes heavily a few times, gasps, and then—

nothing.

"Mommy!" cries my mother. "Don't go, oh no!" And she buries her head on the bed and sobs. It's excruciating. But I force myself to stay. Dad puts his arms around Mom and strokes her, says nothing, kisses the top of her head.

I look at Grandma.

I thought she was gone before, but she is really gone now.

For a while I pace in the waiting room while Mom and Dad pack up her things, talk to the doctors, call the undertaker.

I am useless. Not Mom. I can't believe how together she is.

I can't imagine the world without my mother.

I tell them I'm going out for a walk, and I run down the stairs, down, down, down, all six flights, into the lobby. It's really early in the morning, but the place is bustling, full of nurses coming in for shifts, people coming in for tests. . . . I run out into the parking lot, sobbing, screaming. I run, scream, nobody stops me, says "Are you OK?" I guess they figure someone I love has died.

I run. I run and run. I could run forever.

And then I can't anymore. I can't breathe. Literally breathless, I sit down on a curb. There must be some air here somewhere. I close my eyes, put my head between my knees in case I'm going to faint.

I breathe in and out, in and out. Slowly. Like I am giving myself mouth-to-mouth resuscitation. CPR. But it's not the breaths that are important. It's the pounding on the heart. That's what they told us in a school assembly last year.

So I pound on my heart, like we do at Yom Kippur. Pardon me. Forgive me. Grant me atonement.

I have no idea where I am. I have to call my dad. But just then a car pulls up, the SUV I love to hate.

"Do you want a ride?" the rabbi asks me, leaning his head out the window.

"With you?" I say. "No way. No effin' way."

He turns off the engine, opens the door. Gets out of the car. Walks slowly toward me and sits down next to me.

I inch away from him. I have breath again, enough to say,

"I know what you did, and you are not going to deny it. I heard you."

"Rachel," he says.

"I hate you," I whisper. I look up. He is looking at me, not away. "I hate you!" I say again.

The rabbi sighs.

"I'm sorry about your grandmother," he says.

"You know?"

He nods. "Your father called. I went to the hospital. . . ."

"To be with my mother?" I say. "To be with my mother?" I am kind of screaming now.

"To be with all of you. That's my job. And they said you'd gone out for a walk, so I came looking for you."

I don't have my phone with me.

"Why you, not my father?"

"Your mother wanted him to stay with her."

I let that sink in. A glimmer of hope.

"So that's your job, going to the hospital?"

"Sure. Part of it."

"And what's the other part? Screwing women you're not married to? In the sanctuary? On the *bima*?"

He stares at me.

"What was your *kavanah* with that, Rabbi?"

"What?" he asks.

I wasn't going to do this, I wasn't going to confront him, but here he is and here I am and I guess I'm doing it.

"Come on. Don't play dumb with me. I heard you. One evening before class. You did it with some girl who was going to get married—"

"What? I didn't do anything—"

"Do *not* deny it."

He shakes his head, sighs. Looks at me and then quickly away. "You saw that?"

Heard it. Whatever. "Yup."

"Oy vey. Oh, God. Oh, God, what have I done? Poor Rachel. Poor, poor Rachel, what have I done to you?"

I want to say, You ruined my life, but I know it's not true. "You've made a big mess of things," I tell him. "You've hurt a lot of people, I'm sure. I know you hurt me. You made me—" I don't know what to say except "old."

"Oh, God, forgive me," he mumbles, his head in his hands.

"Yes," I say, "you better atone, Rabbi. Ask that God you love so much for forgiveness."

He bows his head, and I see that he is bald on top, and in spite of myself I laugh. "You've got no hair on top. Is that why you usually wear a *kipah*?"

"You got me," he says, laughing through his tears. "This is why I've always loved you, Rachel, because you can do that— Oh, don't let me have ruined you. Please! Please!"

"You haven't ruined me," I tell him. "You haven't."

"I screwed up," he says.

"Screwed is the right word," I say. "You are really a fucker," I say, furious at him. I am not going to let him win me back.

He bristles and gets all rabbi-like. "Rachel!"

"Don't give me that," I say. "You have lost your right to be holy and superior with me."

He nods and frowns. "OK, you're right. But could you stop with the language, please? Please?"

We sit for a while without talking, and I calm down. He is just a man. He's not a god. Or God's best friend. Or God's best work. I will have to live with that. So will he, I guess.

"I've made some really big mistakes, Rachel," he says. "I'm so sorry you had to see that."

"If you didn't want to hurt me—"

He hears it as a question. "No, not you. You of all people."

"*If* you didn't want to hurt me, then why did you have an affair with my mother? Why did you *ruin* my parents' marriage?"

"No, no! Your mother and I, we didn't have an affair—"

"I saw you kissing her. In my driveway."

"We didn't," he says into his hands. "I swear it. Your mother and I talked a lot. A lot. We kissed only that once. I wanted more, but she didn't."

"Why?"

"You'll have to ask her."

I sit there for a long time. The rabbi sits next to me. Doing nothing else. Just being with me.

"My grandma died," I say. "I am going to miss her so much."

He nods. "I know you will, Rachel. But she's at peace now, finally," he says, and I know that in this case that is the truth.

After a while, I say, "Can you take me to my parents?"

"Sure. Let me find out where they are."

He stands and calls my dad. I hear such a sadness in his voice, and I wonder if it's for me, for my grandmother, or for what he's about to go through. My heart—I cannot stop it—my heart goes out to him. "They're going back home," he tells me.

"Listen," I say. "Before we go. It's Adam. He knows about you and the cheating. He's thinking about doing something crazy. Will you talk to him? Right away? Before he does something really bad?"

The rabbi sits down next to me again. He sighs. "I never meant to hurt him."

"Well, you did!" I say. "You really did. And he wants to get revenge. I think he really could do something terrible."

"Oh my God. I am such a— I'll talk to him right away. I never meant for him to bear the brunt of our— I love that boy so much. Thank you for telling me, Rachel."

"He's really a good guy, Adam is. Or he could be—but . . ."

The rabbi nods, looks at me. "Thank you. Really. I'll talk to him. He'll be fine. I promise."

"OK," I say, hoping I can believe him. And after a few minutes, I ask the rabbi to take me home. "Please?"

"Yes, of course."

I get in the front seat, but we drive in silence.

"What am I going to do now?" I ask the rabbi as he pulls into the driveway.

"You'll grieve," he says. "You'll grieve for what you've lost. And then you'll move on."

We both know he's not talking only about Grandma.

CHAPTER 35

NEW LEAF

We're having the funeral in two days, waiting for all the out-of-town relatives to arrive. This is not what you're supposed to do when you're Jewish. You're supposed to get them buried right away, the very next day. But there are people from far away who really want to come.

I'm sure God will understand.

Dad's a whirlwind of activity, cleaning up the yard and the house. I notice that every once in a while he finds Mom and gives her a hug, a kiss, a cup of tea. And this morning he woke me up without singing but then came and stood by my bed.

"I love you, Rachel," he said, and kissed me on the head.

The doorbell keeps ringing. People are dropping off food. Delivery guys are bringing flowers, fruit baskets. Mrs. Philips is in the kitchen organizing everything. She keeps shooing Mom and me out when we try to help.

In a quiet moment I go to my room and call Alexis. I have to give it one more try. Her phone rings, but she does not pick up.

"Rachel, can you come here?" Mom calls from her bedroom.

"Uh-oh," I say when I see the mess.

"Yup. It's all I could think of to do."

She's got all her clothes heaped on the bed. All of them. Her closet is empty; her drawers are open and most of them are empty, too. Like I said, Uh-oh. People are going to start arriving soon. We can't leave it like this. Mom goes through her clothes every once in a while, and I help her, but I've never seen her do *this*.

She usually ends up with two or more big plastic bags full of clothing that we take to New Leaf, the battered-women's shelter.

I move a few clothes to one side so I can sit on the bed, leaning up against the headboard on Dad's side. Mom's standing up at her dresser, her back to me, rifling through her scarf drawer.

"I know I had the matching scarf to that dress somewhere." She points with her head, and I know she means that striped/flowered/paisley peasant thing that was in for a nanosecond a few years ago.

"You'll find it," I tell her.

"It always gets worse before it gets better," she says.

"Tell me about it," I say, and then sigh.

She turns around and looks at me. "How about you tell me about it," she says.

I shake my head.

"It's time," she says. "For us to talk."

I'm. Not. Ready.

"How about this, Mom? Let me help you with the clothes. People will be here so soon. Just tell me what you're definitely giving away and I'll put it in bags."

"That's the trouble, I'm not sure. I'm not sure who I want to be, what clothes I want to wear. . ."

"Sounds familiar," I say. "But aren't you old enough to, you know, know?"

"I haven't grown up yet, I guess."

Or maybe your mother just died.

"You seem pretty grown-up to me," I say, looking at the streaks of gray in her hair (has she gotten more lately?), the lines around her eyes, around her mouth. I will not think of Grandma in the hospital bed. I will not.

"If you only knew . . . ," Mom says.

"So tell me," I say.

"Not so fast. You first. C'mon, Rachel."

"Don't you— Shouldn't you be thinking about Grandma and stuff?"

"Plenty of time for that. This talk is long overdue."

She moves some clothes away and sits down on the other side of the bed, on her side. We both look out the window. It's a bright late-fall day, almost winter. Most of the leaves are gone from the trees.

She puts her hand on my leg. "I'm ready."

"OK." I can do this. "You know the night you picked me up from confirmation class and I started sobbing in the car?"

"Yeah."

And here I go.

To say she is dumbfounded is putting it mildly.

"What?" she says over and over. "What?"

I keep going.

"Sex, on the *bima*? The rabbi? And you heard? I feel sick to my stomach, Rachel."

"Tell me about it. I threw up afterward. My whole dinner."

"Oh, you poor baby." She reaches over to hug me, but I pull away.

"Not yet, Mom. I need to tell you more."

Mom lets go but stays next to me. "Go on."

I tell her about the bathroom, and the bride. "Oh dear. That was the girl who was supposed to marry Justin Ross, but then she called it off."

"She called it off? Could I have done something, if I had told then?"

"No. NO. That is *not* on you, Rachel. Oh, so much is falling into place. . . . Holy sh—"

"Should I stop for now?"

"No. Keep going. I want to hear it all."

"Well, there's one thing I have to tell you, and ask you," I say to her. "If you can take it."

"First let me ask you, sweetie, why did it take you so long to say something to me?"

"That's the thing, Mom. You *flirted* with him. That night. When we were in the car. I thought, I think, I don't know— I'm worried that—you were or are having an affair with him, Mom. The rabbi." I feel surprisingly calm. It's such a relief, really, to be saying it to her.

Mom doesn't say anything. Not for a long time. I'm beginning to think it is true.

"Oh my God, were you? Are you?"

"No, Rachel. I'm not. I didn't. But—don't freak out—I came close. And everything you've told me has made it all so much clearer."

After a few minutes, I say, "I saw you kiss him."

She sighs.

"In our driveway. Walking home from school, I saw you leaning against the car. His car."

"I was worried you had, but he—the rabbi—convinced me it wasn't, I don't know, physically possible for you or anyone to have seen."

"The man is a major bullshitter," I said.

"Yeah."

"But, Mom, the kiss?"

"Believe it or not—and I know you're going to think I'm not telling the truth, but I swear I am—that was the only time we kissed."

So the rabbi wasn't lying. About that.

"I felt awful about it, Raebee. Awful. But then there was what happened with Grandma and— I told Dad about it, not right away, but I did. It was bumpy for a while, but . . ."

"Are you two going to split up?" I might as well know now.

"I hope not. No. No." And then she turns to me. "Wow, he was seducing women, or trying to, all over town, wasn't he?"

"That's what Adam says. I guess so."

"Shit." Mom looks pained. "Sorry. I'm really upset. I shouldn't curse in front of you."

"Mom," I say. "I heard the rabbi fucking in the sanctuary. I shoplifted and planted it on Alexis. The time to worry about my innocence has passed."

She looks at me, smiles sadly. "True enough."

By the end of the afternoon, I have told my mother pretty much everything, leaving out some of the more intimate and illegal details. When I ask her about Alexis, what she thinks will happen, she gives me a hug and just says, "Time will tell. You never know. If you are meant to be friends, you will be."

Mom has put half of her clothes in the give-away pile. I calmly and quietly suggest that although we put the clothes in bags, we shouldn't take them right over to New Leaf.

"Nope," she says. "They're going now." She looks at me, puts her hand on my shoulder. "It's been a bad couple of years for me, honey. I need to do this today."

And so I help her load all of the stuff into Dad's car.

As we're putting the last bag into the trunk, she looks at me with a smile.

"So, Jacob Schmidt, huh?"

I nod.

"He's a smart boy. And handsome. Not too perfect, is he?"

"No, not too perfect," I say. "Human."

"Good. Be careful of the ones who seem perfect. And how does he feel about you?"

"The same, I think. I hope. I'm not sure."

"If he's as smart as I think he is," she says, grabbing me into a hug, "he'll love you for who you are. Mistakes and all."

She slams the trunk and we get into the car. Before she pulls away, she turns to me and smiles. "Soon you'll be sitting in the driver's seat."

When we get back, there are tons of cars out front. The relatives have arrived. Mom goes in, but I stay outside by myself for a few minutes. We were right near where Randy lived. I can't believe I'll never know what happened to him, how he turned out. I call

Jake, but his phone is off. Is it a school day? I guess it is. I text him. I tell him Grandma died, in case he doesn't know already. I tell him I miss him. And then I tell him I'm turning off my phone so I can sit with my family. To be here with *kavanah*. And I do.

CHAPTER 36

THE SANCTUARY

I don't want to go to my grandmother's funeral. I would rather be almost anywhere else.

I've ducked out of the rabbi's office to go to the bathroom (*the* bathroom!) to splash water on my face. I have been crying pretty much all morning.

I look in the mirror to make sure I look OK. I don't. Or, I guess I look like someone in mourning should look. There's that ripped black ribbon again. In the old days I would have had to rip my clothing. I didn't cringe when the rabbi pinned it on me. Surprisingly. My mother and father seemed to be a little wary of him, though, which I think is a good thing. They thought about asking the new assistant rabbi to do the service, but Rabbi Cohn is the one who knew Grandma. He'll do a good job. He will.

But oh God. Can I go through this again?

I sit down on the couch for a few minutes to pull myself together a little bit. I was so touched when Adam called our house this morning. He said he was very sorry to hear about my grandmother. And he told me that his father has started talking to him. I was worried he would be mad at me, but he wasn't. He said he didn't think his parents would stay married, but he thought that was good.

I asked him if he would tell Alexis about the funeral, tell her I'd like her to come. He said he already had told her, but he'd give her my message. I told him I had texted her but hadn't heard back.

He didn't say anything.

"Jake, too," I said.

"He's a good guy, Rachel," Adam said. "But not too good, I hope?"

"Nah," I laughed.

"Do you think Alexis will come?" I asked Adam.

"No promises," he said. "But I'll try."

"Please tell her I'm truly, deeply sorry. OK?"

"OK," Adam said.

"And that I forgive *her*."

"Rachel, it's time," my dad says now, poking his head in the door.

"OK," I say, and I walk out of the bathroom.

We walk into the sanctuary, Mom between Dad and me. We are all holding hands.

I see Adam sitting in the back row. My new friend, Adam. Who would have thunk it?

But no Alexis. I guess that's it. No Alexis. I can't believe it. But I can't go there now.

I look for Jake but don't see him. He must be here, though. He *must*.

There's Mrs. Glick. Marissa, Kendra. Even McKelvy. That's really nice.

If only I could find Jake.

But I stop looking for him, because there is Grandma's coffin, where Grandpa's was, in front of the *bima*.

My grandma is in there. Closed up in that box. Not my grandma. The thought of her in that box—no!

My gut—I can't. But I have to. Oh, God, please help me. Tears stream down my face.

Mom, Dad, and I sit in the front row with the rest of the family. Right next to the coffin.

And then, just as the rabbi walks onto the *bima* to start the service and I think I can't bear this, I feel a hand on my shoulder. I turn around.

It's Jake. He is sitting right behind me.

The Sanctuary, Now

I look at the *bima*, the stained-glass windows, the memorial wall. My grandparents' names are up there. It seems so long ago, and yet not. When Mom and Dad told me at the end of that year that we were moving to New York, I was devastated. I didn't want to leave Jake, or my new friends. But the move turned out to be good for my parents and for me. Jake and I—it was bumpy for a while, but we are together. Forever.

And now we might be moving back here. If I get the job.

I hear voices in the lobby, footsteps. My interview—

The sanctuary door opens.

"Rabbi?" someone says.

"Yes," I say. "Here I am."

ACKNOWLEDGMENTS

When you've worked on a book as long as I've worked on this one (for years I referred to it as my book-in-a-box), you have a whole universe of people to thank. Given that, I'm afraid I may forget someone, so if I do, please forgive me. It was not intentional.

I started this book during President Bill Clinton's second administration. So probably I should thank him. But I don't think I will. However, I would like to thank people who helped me during those early days, most especially the women in my Pennsylvania writers' group, the Bucks County Authors of Books for Children: Joyce McDonald (who read an early draft and gave me great comments), Pat Brisson, Martha Hewson, Pamela Jane, Sally Keehn, Susan Korman, Wendy Pfeffer, Pamela Curtis Swallow, Kay Winters, and Elvira Woodruff. These women have been my lifeline for years.

Bunny Gabel, legendary teacher of children's book writing at the New School, gave me great feedback and encouragement, as did the members of her class. If it hadn't been for Bunny, I might have left the book in a box. Thanks also to Lucy Frank, Marguerite Holloway, Patty Lakin, Laurent Linn, Roxane Orgill, Erika Tamar, Marfé Delano, and Elizabeth Winthrop for critiques and helpful talks along the way. Thanks to the Henry's gang. And to Suzannah Hershkowitz.

These brilliant writers and dear friends read near-final drafts of the book, and I am greatly indebted to them for their insightful suggestions (even if I didn't take every one) and for their sustaining friendship: Laurie Halse Anderson, Judy Blundell, Barbara Kerley, Susan Kuklin, and Rebecca Stead. I am so blessed to have each of them as a friend and a reader. They make the journey fun, easier, and truly nourishing.

Nancy Sandberg knows what it is to be a friend. My friend.

I have rabbis to thank. Rabbi Berlin said exactly the right thing when my mother died. Rabbi Shira Stern and Rabbi Don Weber talked with me many times over the years about this book, gave me insights about being a rabbi, and then read a near-final draft. They caught some mistakes (ram, *not* goat!) and encouraged me in ways that made it possible to actually publish the thing. I would also like to thank the late Rabbi Sandy Roth for teaching me new things about Judaism, most especially about *kavannah.* One Yom Kippur she handed out a card I keep in my wallet at all times. On one side it says, "The world was created for me." On the other, "I am dust." From her to me to you.

Where would I be without Ken Wright? Under the desk, in the box, with the many drafts. There is no way I can thank him enough, but I'll try. Here goes: you are effing amazing, Mr. Wright. Thank you for your encouragement, your nudges, your understanding, your humor, your DH, your Link, your friendship, and—most especially—your faith in me. I bow down as well to

Kristy King, whom I forgive, just barely, for moving to California, and to Jenna Shaw, who has a sharp eye and a kind heart, and to Amanda Williams, who keeps things going now at Writers House.

Gargantuan thanks to my incredible editor, Michelle Frey. Wow. (And to think she graduated from Brown with a degree in religious studies. Where would *that* degree get you?) Michelle is one awesome editor, and if I weren't terrified of heights, I would shout it from the rooftop of the Random House building. So just consider this that shout. I will be forever grateful to her for helping me sculpt the mess she received into—a book. Many thanks also to Kelly Delaney for everything she did for Rachel, for me, for Michelle and for the book. An almost speechless thank-you to the designers of *the most beautiful cover in the universe*, Christian Fuenfhausen and Cathy Bobak. You are virtuosic. And I bow down to copy editors Artie Bennett and Jennifer Healey. I am a terrible speller, awful at commas, and pretty much a writer *made* for copy editors. Thank you for saving my butt. Thanks to Michele Burke, who read an early draft and made great suggestions, and to Nancy Hinkel, the publishing director of Alfred A. Knopf Books for Young Readers.

Thanks to my whole family, both born-into and married-into. And a particular thanks to my niece, Natalie Sams, for reading the manuscript, loving it, and being walloped. Sorry, but thanks.

To my sons Aaron and Benjamin: thank you for your love and support, your teasing, and your general awesomeness at loving me and keeping me grounded. Also for your terrific smarts. Aaron, if you knew what was good for you, though, you'd let me win a little more often in Scrabble. Benjamin, thank you for a great reading of the book. Oh, and definitely pretzels. Always pretzels.

My husband, Jonathan, has stood by me and this book for*ever*. It's impossible for me to exaggerate his importance in my life as a friend, a reader, and a husband. And here's how sweet he is: after he read a draft, he made me the exact meal Jake makes for Rachel. And he's not even a cook.

I'd like to thank Rachel and Jake and Adam. Thanks for sticking with me. Now off you go.

Deborah Heiligman's *Charles and Emma* received many accolades including a Printz Honor Award and five starred reviews, and was a National Book Award finalist. *Publishers Weekly* called it "rewarding" and "illuminating," and *Booklist* named it a Top 10 Youth Romance title. Deborah lived in Pennsylvania for many years and now lives in New York City with her husband. Find out more about Deborah at deborahheiligman.com.